CW01642777

LITTLE ONE

FIONA HOLLOWAY

BLACK SWAN
DIGITAL

First published in 2025
Concept created by Black Swan Digital. Developed by Mark Coleman.

PROLOGUE

The crib is perfect. The white, polished wood gleams like bone in the half-light. I run my hands along the smooth, unblemished bars, pausing at a minuscule splinter in the grain. That won't do. A child's delicate hands might catch on it, might bleed. I pinch it free with my nails and press it into my palm, letting it prick sharply against my skin.

The nursery smells of lavender and starch. Freshly laundered sheets are neatly folded and stacked in the dresser. The wallpaper, a faded buttercup yellow, peels slightly at the corners, curling like old parchment. I smooth it down. Everything must be just so.

On the shelf above the changing table, stuffed animals sit in orderly rows, their button eyes glassy, unblinking. A velveteen rabbit. A plush bear with a drooping ear. A doll with painted lashes and a thin red mouth, her hands forever outstretched, as if waiting for something, someone, to hold.

The chair in the corner rocks gently as I pass. A trick of the wind, surely, yet my breath catches. I stop, listening. The house is quiet but not empty. Never empty. Houses, after all, remember things. They hold whispers in their walls, keep traces of those who have passed through them, like flowers pressed between pages.

I lean into the crib, running my hands over the mattress. It's softer than I expected, dipping slightly under the weight of my palm. I press harder, flattening it. No lumps, no uneven spots. A child should sleep soundly, undisturbed.

I reach for the handmade quilt, each stitch perfect. I spent hours on it, pricking my fingers raw, letting little red blooms soak into the fabric. But the color was wrong. Too bright. I had to start over. This one is better, softer, a muted blue. Calming. The color of a pale morning sky, the hush before the day begins.

I lift the quilt to my face and inhale deeply. It smells of linen, of cold air, and something faintly metallic, something beneath the surface that I can't quite name. The taste of a memory, just out of reach.

Almost ready.

I move to the window. Outside, the world is dim and waiting, the trees skeletal against the dusk. The wind sighs through the branches, rattling the shutters. A leaf scrapes across the glass making a dry, brittle sound that makes the hairs on my arms rise.

I place my hand against my stomach.

Flat.

My fingers press into the silk of my dress, feeling the hard planes of my ribs beneath. A dull, hollow ache blooms inside me, not pain exactly, but absence.

Once, long ago, I had a shape inside me. A small, growing thing. A weight beneath my skin, shifting, stretching. I would place my hand there and feel the flutter and the pulse of something new and unfinished.

Now, there is only stillness.

Sadly inevitable, they told me. These things happen. Bodies betray us. Fate unwinds in cruel, careless ways.

But I know better.

I close my eyes, letting the hush of the room settle around me. Shadows stretch long across the floorboards. The wind presses against the glass in gentle, shushing gusts. The whole house is quiet, listening.

In the corner, the mobile turns.

Tiny silver stars spin slowly, catching the light. A lullaby plays in my head, low and sweet, the notes curling around me like fingers. My mother used to sing it to me when I was small, pressing her lips to my temple, her breath warm against my skin.

I imagine small hands reaching for the stars, grasping them and tiny fingers wrapping around nothing. I imagine breath, steady and rhythmic, the soft rise and fall of a chest, the fragile weight of a body nestled against mine.

I imagine the moment I hear the first cry, the first gasp of air, the first time I will hold them close, feel their warmth seep into me, filling all the hollow spaces.

It will happen. It has to.

I exhale softly and whisper, "Soon, little one. Very soon."

The wind rattles the shutters. The rocking chair creaks once then stills.

I step back, surveying the room one last time. The mobile continues its slow, steady spin. The stuffed animals stare, their stitched smiles unchanging. The crib stands silent, empty. Waiting.

I press my palm flat against my stomach one last time.

The ache deepens.

The house settles around me, shifting with the weight of night. Somewhere in the distance, a branch snaps creating a hollow sound, like something breaking.

I turn, flick off the light, and close the door behind me.

1

PRESENT

Seven years have passed, but time has been kind to me, or at least, that's what I tell myself. The past lingers like a shadow at the edges of my mind, but I have learned to live in the light. I have a husband who loves me, a son who needs me, and a life that, from the outside, looks just like everyone else's on this street.

We – the Warrens – live in a two-story home with navy siding and white shutters, nestled neatly in a cul-de-sac in a town just outside Richmond, Virginia. It's the kind of house I used to stare at in magazines, the kind that makes you think of lemonade on the porch in summer and pumpkin wreaths on the door in fall. The windows have thick white trim, and the front door is painted a soft shade of blue that Dan picked out himself. There's a garden out front, one I keep meaning to tend to more often, but the roses seem to bloom just fine without my help.

Inside, the house smells of fresh coffee and warm vanilla, scents that make it feel like home. Sunlight filters through the bay window in the living room, casting golden streaks across the wooden floors. Picture frames line the hallway, the snapshots of a life I have built from the ground up. One from our wedding day, my lace dress billowing in the breeze, Dan looking at me as if I were something worth holding onto. Another from the day Noah was born, his tiny face scrunched up, his fist curled tightly around my finger. A hundred memories, frozen in time remain as proof that I have moved on, that I have survived.

Dan is at the kitchen table, flipping through the morning paper. He still insists on reading the print edition, says the ink smudging his fingertips is part of the experience. His coffee sits untouched beside him, steam curling from the rim. He's solid and steady, everything I could have hoped for in a husband. A man who doesn't flinch at the cracks in me. A man who sees the ghosts in my eyes and chooses to stay anyway.

Noah is three now, all wild curls and dimpled hands, a hurricane of energy wrapped in soft cotton pajamas. He is always moving, always talking, always finding new ways to make a mess. Right now, he's perched on the floor, stacking blocks into a precarious tower. His tongue peeks out in concentration, his little fingers carefully placing one block on top of the other.

"Look, Mama," he says, beaming up at me. "It's gonna reach the sky."

I smile and crouch beside him, brushing a stray curl from his forehead. "You're going to need a lot more blocks for that."

He giggles and topples the tower over, delighted by the crash. Dan glances up from his paper, smirking. "Engineer in the making," he says, taking a sip of his coffee.

I sip my own, letting the bitter warmth spread through me. It's a ritual that grounds me in this life I've built. The ceramic mug is smooth beneath my fingers, a gift from Noah on Mother's Day, decorated with his tiny handprints in bright blue paint. I run my thumb over the smudged edges of perfect imperfection, a reminder that he's growing too fast.

The kitchen is the heart of our home, with its white cabinets and marble countertops, and an island where Noah likes to sit and watch me cook. A chalkboard hangs on the wall, a running grocery list scribbled across it in Dan's neat handwriting mixed with my scrawled reminders and Noah's wobbly drawings. The fridge is cluttered with magnets and notes, birthday invitations and preschool artwork. A chaotic collage of our daily life.

The house is always filled with sound. Noah's laughter, the noise of the dishwasher, the low murmur of Dan on the phone with a client. But sometimes, when the world settles into stillness, when the night presses in and the past stirs in the corners of my mind, I wonder if it's all too perfect. If I have built something too fragile, too good to last.

There are nights when I wake up with the sheets damp and twisted around my legs, heart hammering, the echo of a child's laughter slipping away into the dark. I tell myself they're only dreams. That the past is a place I no longer live.

And yet, some part of me knows the past never really stays buried. It lingers, waiting for the right moment to claw its way back to the surface.

But for now, I breathe in the scent of coffee, listen to Noah giggle as he builds his tower again, and watch Dan chuckle at something absurd in the news.

Dan is the kind of man people trust. Maybe it's the way he carries himself with his shoulders squared, and a quiet confidence that makes people believe he knows what he's doing. Or maybe it's the steady voice, measured, reassuring, as if even the worst news could be softened by the way he says it. It's probably why he's so good at what he does.

Dan is a defense attorney. A good one. The kind that makes juries lean in when he speaks, that makes witnesses shift uncomfortably under his scrutiny. He built his career on precision, on logic, on knowing how to read people. It's a skill that never turns off, not even at home. I've caught him watching me sometimes, a slight crease in his brow, as if trying to decipher something unspoken. It doesn't bother me. Not really. He doesn't push, doesn't ask questions I'm not ready to answer. That's what I love about him. He lets me exist exactly as I am, ghosts and all.

Our house sits right at the end of the cul-de-sac. Our sanctuary, with a front porch swing that creaks when the wind moves just right. A row of sycamores lines the street, their branches bending toward one another as if sharing secrets. In the fall, their leaves cover the pavement in gold and rust, and Noah loves nothing more than jumping into freshly raked piles, scattering them like confetti.

The backyard is Noah's kingdom, filled with chalk drawings that wash away with the rain, a red plastic slide that wobbles slightly when he climbs too high, and a battered sandbox where he buries toy dinosaurs. At night, when the cicadas hum and fireflies flicker, Dan and I sit on the porch steps, listening to the sounds of our neighborhood settling in for the night. It's peaceful. Ordinary. Everything I never thought I'd have.

I met Dan on a rainy Thursday in a coffee shop just outside the city. I was drowning in paperwork, my laptop balanced precariously on my knees, a cold cup of tea forgotten beside me. He sat across from me, a stranger then, watching as I muttered under my breath at a particularly stubborn document.

"You know, talking to it probably won't make it cooperate," he had said, his voice laced with amusement.

I looked up, ready to glare, but something about the way he smiled was easy, unguarded and made my irritation fizzle out.

We talked for hours that day, the rain streaking the windows, the coffee shop emptying around us. He asked questions that made me think, listened like he actually cared about the answers. He made me laugh when I hadn't remembered how in a long time. By the time we left, the city slick with rain, he had already tucked himself into the corners of my mind.

Marrying Dan felt like stepping into the sun after years of cold. He never asked me about my past. Not the way others did. He never pried, never pushed, never made me feel like a story he was trying to unravel. He simply accepted that there were parts of me that might always remain closed off, and that was enough for him.

Noah abandons his tower now, rubbing sleep from his eyes, his curls a mess of golden-brown tangles. He climbs onto Dan's lap, curling into his chest, and Dan presses a kiss to his temple, murmuring something low and soothing. My heart tugs at the sight of them. It is an easy, quiet love, full of warmth I never thought I'd be part of.

I move to the stove, flipping pancakes, the scent of butter and vanilla filling the air. Noah watches me sleepily, his head tucked under Dan's chin.

"Pancakes, buddy?" Dan asks, ruffling his hair.

Noah nods, groggy and snuggling, and I smile as I slide the first pancake onto his plate. This is what mornings are now. They are soft and golden, stitched together with laughter and the clinking of forks against plates.

I know how lucky I am. I know how fragile happiness can be. But for now, in this house filled with warmth and love and the scent of pancakes, I let myself believe it will last.

Because that's what you do when you have everything to lose. You hold on with both hands and hope.

The day moves slowly in the best kind of way. The kind where soft light filters through the kitchen window, catching dust motes in the air, where the distant sound of a lawnmower somewhere in the neighborhood becomes the background music to a relaxed, easy morning.

Noah has been outside most of the morning, alternating between the sandbox and the slide, chattering to himself in that earnest, thoughtful way only three-year-olds do. Every now and then, he runs inside with a new discovery like a pebble he's convinced is special, a caterpillar inching its way across his palm, or a dandelion he insists I blow for him.

Dan left for work after breakfast, straightening his tie in the mirror before pressing a kiss to my forehead. "Try to relax today," he said, giving my waist a gentle squeeze before heading out the door. He worries about me sometimes, even if he doesn't say it.

I hear the low purr of Claire's car engine before I see it pulling into the driveway. A moment later, the doorbell rings letting out two sharp chimes, followed by her voice. "I bring gifts!" she calls.

I wipe my hands on a dish towel and head for the door. When I swing it open, Claire is standing there, grinning with a bottle of Sauvignon Blanc dangling from one hand, a brown paper bag from the deli down the street in the other.

"Lunch and wine?" I raise an eyebrow. "Are you proposing to me?"

She laughs, brushing past me into the house. "I figured you could use a little midday indulgence," she says, setting the bag on the counter. "And let's be real, you never say no to a crisp glass of white."

She's not wrong.

Claire is a whirlwind. The kind of woman who takes up space in the best possible way. She's blonde and curvy, with a laugh that could shake the rafters, and she moves through life with an ease I sometimes envy. She's been here for almost two years now, but it feels like longer, like she was always meant to be a part of my life, like I had been waiting for her without even realizing it.

We met by chance in a bookstore of all places. I was

lingering by the crime fiction section, running my fingers over the spines without really seeing them, when we reached for the same book at the same time.

"Oh, this one is twisted in the best way," she had said, pulling it down and pressing it into my hands. I had laughed, and somehow, we ended up in the café next door, just two strangers swapping life stories over lattes.

Now, she's my person. My best friend.

She adores Noah, and he worships her in return. She spoils him in ways I don't, by sneaking him sweets when she thinks I'm not looking, letting him stay up past bedtime when she babysits, teaching him silly songs that he sings for days afterward.

And Dan? Dan thinks she's hilarious. They banter like siblings, trading jabs over dinner, and sometimes, I catch him looking at me across the table like he's grateful I have her.

She plucks two wine glasses from the cabinet, already making herself at home, as she always does. "How's my favorite little guy?" she calls toward the backyard.

There's a quick patter of feet before Noah bursts through the screen door, beaming.

"Claire!" he squeals, running straight into her legs.

She scoops him up easily, peppering his cheeks with exaggerated kisses. "God, you get cuter every day," she says, hugging him tight. "Tell me, has your mother been treating you well? Or has she been depriving you of all the sugar and joy you deserve?"

Noah giggles, his fingers tangling in her hair. "She made pancakes."

Claire gasps, setting him down. "Pancakes? What a terrible, awful mother you have." She turns to me with mock seriousness. "I can't believe you would feed him something so delightful and nutritious. I am disappointed."

I roll my eyes, pouring the wine. "Sit down and eat your sandwich."

She grins, grabbing her glass and following me to the table. Noah clambers onto his chair, already reaching for his juice box, his legs swinging beneath him.

This is what life is now.

Easy. Full. Safe.

And yet, sometimes, when the house is quiet and the night stretches long, I still feel the lingering shadow of something I can't quite name.

But right now, in the middle of the day, with Noah's laughter ringing through the kitchen and Claire's bright energy filling the room, I can almost forget.

Almost.

2

EIGHT YEARS AGO

The drive to Lockwood Estate was longer than Isabel had anticipated. The winding coastal road stretched endlessly ahead, bordered on one side by towering pine trees and on the other by sheer cliffs that plunged into the wild, frothing sea. The sky above was a bruised shade of early evening, streaked with the last wisps of daylight, and the air was thick with the scent of salt and damp earth.

Isabel's hands clenched the steering wheel, her palms clammy despite the chill. She wasn't a nervous person by nature, at least, not outwardly. But this was different. This was the Lockwood family. A name that carried weight, evoking images of old money and veiled scandals, whispered about in hushed conversations over cocktails. She had worked as a nanny before, of course, but never in a house like this, and never for people like them. She had spent the last three nights lying awake in her tiny apartment, poring over articles, trying to decipher the puzzle that was Oliver and Evelyn Lockwood.

The estate's wrought-iron gates loomed suddenly in her headlights, tall and imposing, like something out of a gothic novel. They groaned as they swung open, granting her entry, and she drove slowly up the gravel path, the crunch of stones beneath her tires breaking the otherwise perfect silence.

The house emerged through the trees like an opulent monstrosity of stone and ivy, its symmetrical façade reminiscent of the grand estates of old New England. It stood three stories high, its tall windows gleaming gold in the dying light, their intricate trim lending the place an air of cold elegance.

She parked beside a black sedan, her heart hammering, and took a steadying breath before stepping out of the car. Her heels sank slightly into the gravel as she adjusted the strap of her bag, smoothing her skirt. At twenty-five, she was old enough to know better than to let herself be intimidated, yet there was something about this house, something about the weight of its history, that made her feel like an imposter before she had even stepped inside.

The front doors were towering, deep mahogany, and just as she reached for the knocker, they swung open before she could touch it. The butler, a short man in his fifties, stepped back, allowing her entry.

"Miss Carter, I presume." He smiled, the crow's feet around his eyes deepening. "Please, follow me."

Still clutching her case, Isabel followed like a puppy, trying not to be overwhelmed by the grandeur of the house's interior.

When they reached a large oak door on the far side of the living room, the man knocked. A small boy with dark curls pushed the door open and stood in the threshold, peering up at her with unsettlingly intelligent eyes. Theo Lockwood. Five years old. Isabel had memorized his face from the photographs she'd been sent.

A moment later, a smaller figure appeared beside him, clinging to his side. Charlotte, just three, was a perfect porcelain doll of a child, her golden hair cascading in delicate waves.

"Theo, darling, let Miss Carter inside."

The voice that spoke was cool and composed, belonging to the woman now standing in the hallway. Evelyn Lockwood. She was breathtaking in that cold, effortless way some women possessed. She was tall, slender, her features sharp enough to cut. Dressed in an emerald silk blouse and tailored trousers, she looked more like a statue than a mother, her expression unreadable as she regarded Isabel.

Isabel swallowed and stepped inside. "It's wonderful to meet you, Mrs. Lockwood."

Evelyn's lips curved slightly, a ghost of a smile. "I appreciate you coming on such short notice. I trust you've read the children's schedules?"

"Yes, of course." Isabel's gaze flickered to the children, then back to their mother. "I'm looking forward to getting to know them."

Evelyn took a slow sip of wine from a delicate glass. "We'll see how it goes."

She didn't offer a tour, didn't ask Isabel about herself. She just turned and disappeared into the depths of the house, leaving Isabel alone with Theo and Charlotte.

Theo regarded her for a moment, then held out his hand to present her with his toy. "Do you like dinosaurs?"

Isabel knelt to his level, smiling. "I love dinosaurs."

He considered this, then nodded approvingly. Charlotte, still silent, slipped her tiny hand into Isabel's free one, her grip surprisingly firm.

"Come on," Theo said, leading her toward the stairs. "We'll show you your room."

She followed them up the grand staircase, its polished wood gleaming beneath the warm glow of a chandelier. The corridors were adorned with oil paintings, their gilded frames catching the light, and the air carried the faint scent of old books and something floral, something expensive. The house was silent, unnervingly so, save for the soft padding of their footsteps against the thick Persian runner beneath them.

Theo stopped before a plain wooden door, starkly different from the intricately carved ones they had passed. He pushed it open, revealing a modest room with a narrow bed, a dresser, and a single window overlooking the side gardens. The walls were bare, the bedding simple white linen, the furniture functional but unremarkable. It was clean, it was practical, but it was nothing like the rest of the house.

Isabel stepped inside, her stomach twisting slightly. It was clear this was not a guest's room, nor a part of the house meant to impress. This was a servant's quarters, a quiet reminder of her place in the household.

She dropped her bag onto the bed, exhaling slowly. "It's lovely," she said, forcing a smile.

Theo climbed onto the bed, his small hands pressing into the mattress. Charlotte followed, perching at the edge, her large blue eyes never leaving Isabel as she unpacked. The children sat still, watching as she removed her neatly folded clothes and arranged them in the dresser drawers.

Their unwavering stillness unsettled her. Most children she had cared for fidgeted, grew bored, asked endless questions. But these two remained perfectly poised, their backs straight, their gazes fixed.

She turned to Theo, hoping to break the silence. "Do you like living here?"

He blinked, tilting his head slightly. "Of course. We have everything we need."

Charlotte nodded though her expression was unreadable.

A prickle of unease crept along Isabel's spine. They were polite, articulate, obedient. And yet something about them felt too measured, too rehearsed. As if they had been taught not just how to behave, but how to perform.

Isabel folded the last of her clothes and closed the drawer, forcing a smile. "Well, I think we're going to have a lot of fun together."

Neither child responded. They simply continued to watch her, their faces placid, unreadable.

They remained silent as Isabel finished unpacking, then led her to the pristine nursery. The wooden shelves gleamed, each toy arranged with meticulous precision, the rocking horse positioned at an exact angle near the window. The room carried a faint scent of beeswax and jasmine. It was a fragrance Isabel would soon begin to associate with the Lockwood Estate.

She had spent the last hour playing with Theo and Charlotte, or rather, attempting to. The children were polite and obedient, but distant. They engaged in games only briefly before their gazes flickered toward the large grandfather clock standing against the far wall. Isabel followed their eyes, noting the time. Five fifty-six.

"Shall we play one more game before dinner?" she suggested.

Theo shook his head. "No. We must have tea at six."

His tone was firm, matter-of-fact. Charlotte nodded in silent agreement, her small hands smoothing the folds of her dress.

Isabel hesitated. In other homes, children would beg for a few more minutes of play, trying to delay bath time or dinner. But these two accepted their schedule with eerie discipline.

"Alright then," Isabel said, standing. "Where do we eat?"

"Follow us," Theo said, reaching for Charlotte's hand. Together, they led Isabel out of the nursery and into the dimly lit corridor. The house felt cavernous as they walked, their footsteps swallowed by thick carpets. The walls were lined with dark portraits, the oil-painted figures staring out with unreadable expressions.

As they descended the grand staircase, the scent of

something rich and buttery drifted through the air. Isabel's stomach twisted when she suddenly realized she hadn't eaten since breakfast.

They passed a large, open doorway leading to an elegant dining room, its vast mahogany table set with polished silverware and flickering candlelight. It was the kind of room meant for hosting dignitaries, not feeding children.

Charlotte barely glanced at it. "That's where Mummy and Daddy eat."

Isabel frowned. "Where do you eat?"

Theo pointed ahead, toward a smaller, less adorned room at the end of the corridor.

Before they could reach it, a figure stepped into view. Oliver Lockwood.

Tall and broad-shouldered, he was impeccably dressed in a dark suit, his phone pressed to his ear. He barely acknowledged them as he strode past, his expression unreadable, his voice a low murmur of businesslike efficiency. He didn't glance at the children, didn't even seem to register their presence.

Isabel watched him disappear down another corridor before turning back to Theo and Charlotte. If they were affected by their father's indifference, they didn't show it.

"This way," Theo said, leading her onward.

As Isabel stepped into the children's dining room, she couldn't shake the thought that in this grand, exquisite house, Theo and Charlotte seemed more like carefully placed ornaments than children.

The children's dining room was starkly different from the grandeur of the main dining hall. Smaller and simpler, it featured a sturdy oak table set for three. The lighting was dim, the air thick with the faint scent of aged wood and something cooking in the adjoining kitchen.

Isabel hesitated in the doorway, but Theo and Charlotte

moved forward with purpose, climbing into their chairs with an almost mechanical grace.

The door at the back of the room swung open, and a woman appeared, carrying a heavy silver tray. She was stout, her apron slightly askew, deep lines etched into her tired face. Wisps of dull brown hair framed her round cheeks, and her eyes, though kind, held the weary look of someone who had spent a lifetime in service.

She set the tray down carefully before looking at Isabel. "You must be Miss Carter."

Her voice was gravelly, worn down by years of speaking softly so as not to disturb.

"I'm Mrs. Beckett, the cook."

Isabel extended a hand instinctively, but Mrs. Beckett merely nodded, brushing her hands against her apron before uncovering the dishes.

Steam drifted upward as she lifted the lids, revealing delicate portions of roasted chicken, boiled potatoes, and a medley of vegetables arranged in neat, careful piles. Everything looked precise, portioned with exactness, as if any deviation would be an offense. Isabel's stomach twisted again at the sight of food.

"Miss Carter, you'll be eating with the children," Mrs. Beckett said gently, though her tone left no room for argument. "Mr. and Mrs. Lockwood take their meals separately."

Isabel nodded and lowered herself into the chair between Theo and Charlotte. A plate was placed in front of her, identical to the children's, yet something about the arrangement felt formal and unnatural.

Mrs. Beckett lingered for a moment, smoothing the edges of her apron. "You'll find it's best not to upset the routine," she added in a quieter tone, her eyes flickering toward the children before returning to Isabel. "They don't like change."

Theo lifted his fork, cutting into his chicken with practiced efficiency, Charlotte following suit with silent precision, which was an unsettling trait in a three-year-old. Their table manners were impeccable. Too impeccable. Every movement was deliberate, calculated. They didn't fidget, didn't spill a single crumb. There were no requests for more, no complaints about the food's temperature. Isabel had never seen children so disciplined, so eerily composed.

She cleared her throat, attempting to bridge the growing sense of unease. "Did you both have a good day?"

Theo nodded once. "It was fine."

Charlotte didn't respond, simply continuing to eat in small, measured bites.

Isabel glanced at Mrs. Beckett, but the cook had turned away, busying herself with wiping down the counter.

"You must be hungry, Miss Carter," Theo said suddenly, his voice light yet strangely devoid of true curiosity. "You should eat before it gets cold."

Isabel hesitated, then picked up her fork, the weight of Mrs. Beckett's warning settling over her like a heavy blanket.

It was best not to upset the routine.

~

The sun was sinking, bleeding molten gold into the horizon and casting long shadows over the dense trees lining the Lockwood estate. A car idled just beyond the heavy iron gates, its engine growling in the hush of evening.

Inside, a woman gripped the steering wheel, her knuckles white, her breath coming in uneven bursts.

She had been here too long. Too long watching nothing, staring at the unyielding wrought iron as if sheer will alone could force the house beyond into view. But she knew it was there. She could feel it looming, cold, full of secrets.

Her lips curled as she spat a curse under her breath, her foot jabbing at the brake with impatient force. “That awful woman,” she muttered, her voice thick with loathing. The words came again, sharper this time.

“That awful, awful woman.”

She scrubbed a hand over her face, fingers tangling in her unkempt hair. A dull ache throbbed behind her eyes. A sharp pulse of something old and ugly.

She hadn’t meant to stop here. Hadn’t meant to let herself be drawn back to this place, this memory. And yet, here she was. Again. Watching. Waiting. Burning with something between fury and desperation.

A sharp gust of wind rattled the trees, their leaves whispering a sound like laughter. Her breath hitched. The weight of the night pressed in closer, the estate standing silent, impassive and indifferent to her presence.

She slammed a hand against the wheel. “Goddamn it.”

The outburst sent her pulse into a gallop. Her heart was a fist hammering against her ribs.

She shouldn’t be here. She had no reason to be. But something gnawed at the edges of her resolve in a clawing, insistent need to see, to know, to remind herself that this was not over. Not yet.

With a jerky motion, she shoved the car into gear. Tires screeched against the tarmac as she pulled away, the night swallowing the vehicle whole.

But even as she disappeared down the empty road, her presence lingered like a phantom. A warning.

3

PRESENT

The afternoon drifts by in that golden, lazy way that makes me wish time could stand still, just for a little while longer. Claire and I have done what we do best. Talked too much, laughed too loud, and polished off the rest of the wine without even noticing.

Noah has spent most of it darting between us and the backyard, returning every so often with flushed cheeks and sweaty curls, pressing into me like a small, sun-warmed thing before bouncing away again.

Now, as the light outside shifts, stretching long shadows across the walls, I move around the kitchen, finishing dinner preparations while Claire perches on a stool, flipping idly through a magazine she probably has no intention of reading.

"What time's Dan home?" she asks, swirling the last sip of wine in her glass.

"Soon," I say, glancing at the clock.

As if on cue, I hear the familiar sound of his car pulling into the driveway, the crunch of tires over loose gravel. A moment later, the front door opens, and the scent of aftershave and cool evening air drifts into the house with him.

"Hello, hello," Dan calls, his voice warm and easy.

Noah barrels through the house like a tiny stampede, his bare feet slapping against the hardwood as he launches himself into Dan's legs, wrapping his arms around them with an excited squeal.

Dan lifts him effortlessly, pressing a kiss to his temple. "Hey, buddy. Did you have a good day?"

Noah nods, his curls bouncing as he wriggles happily in Dan's arms. "Claire came!" he announces, as if Dan hasn't known her for nearly two years.

Dan grins. "Did she now? And did she spoil you rotten as usual?"

Noah doesn't answer, but Claire winks at me from her spot at the counter.

"Just a little," she says, not even pretending to be apologetic.

Dan shakes his head in mock disapproval and sets Noah down, ruffling his hair before stepping fully into the kitchen.

That's when he produces the envelope. He places it neatly on the kitchen island. My name is printed on the front in careful, deliberate letters.

"This was outside," he says absently. "No stamp. Probably just one of those neighborhood things."

I glance at it briefly before turning my focus back to cooking. He moves behind me, looping his arms around my waist as I drain the pasta and toss it in the pan with the sauce.

"Smells amazing," he murmurs, pressing his lips against my temple.

I smile, leaning into him. "Your son requested pasta."

Dan glances at Noah, now sitting on the floor, playing with a stray toy car. "Big surprise there."

Claire sighs dramatically. "I don't know how you can eat carbs and still look so annoyingly good," she says, pouring herself another glass of wine.

Dan smirks. "It's a gift."

I roll my eyes, shoving a dish into his hands. "Set the table, oh gifted one."

By the time we all sit down, the kitchen is filled with warmth, the scent of garlic and tomatoes thick in the air. The softness of the evening settles around us, and for a moment, I let myself sink into it.

Dan twirls his fork into his pasta, sighing with satisfaction before shooting me a look. "Alright, your turn first. What did I miss today?"

I take a sip of wine, savoring its crispness before launching into the rundown. "Noah started the day by digging up half the flower bed because, in his words, 'dinosaurs need homes, too.'"

Dan raises an eyebrow at Noah, who is more focused on slurping noodles than participating in the conversation. "That true, buddy?"

Noah nods solemnly. "T-Rex was cold."

Dan bites back a grin. "Ah. Well, in that case, fair enough."

I continue, leaning back in my chair. "Then we had a very dramatic standoff over whether pajamas are acceptable daywear —he insisted they are, I respectfully disagreed."

"Who won?" Dan asks.

Claire snorts into her wine glass. "Take a wild guess."

Dan chuckles, shaking his head. "You're unstoppable, aren't you, bud?"

Noah grins, a string of cheese stretching from his mouth to his plate.

Dan turns back to me. "And you? What did you two do all day?"

I glance at Claire, smirking. "Oh, you know. Solved world hunger, discussed politics, debated the meaning of life."

Claire waves a dismissive hand. "Mostly just drank wine and judged celebrities from the comfort of your couch."

Dan smirks. "Sounds productive."

"What about you?" I ask, nudging his foot under the table. "How was work?"

Dan sighs, swirling his wine. "Busy. Had a client freak out in the middle of a deposition. He started yelling about how the system is corrupt and that he'd rather rot in jail than 'be a pawn in their game.'"

Claire perks up. "Ooh. Drama."

Dan laughs dryly. "Oh, yeah. Real dramatic. Except now I get to spend tomorrow trying to convince a judge my client isn't completely unhinged."

I wince. "That sounds exhausting."

"It is," he says, rubbing his temple before reaching for my hand across the table. "But coming home to this? This makes it all worth it."

The conversation ebbs and flows, laughter punctuating the air, the clinking of silverware filling the spaces between words.

I love the buzz of conversation, the way Noah's little fingers leave smudges on the rim of his juice glass. I love how Dan's presence steadies a room, how Claire fits into our life so seamlessly, like she was always meant to be here.

Because tonight, everything feels exactly as it should.

The scent of dinner lingers leaving traces of garlic, warm tomatoes, the faintest hint of wine in the air. The plates are scraped clean, Noah's small fork abandoned beside his half-finished juice.

Dan carries him upstairs, murmuring bedtime stories as he goes, his voice a low, soothing hum. Claire and I remain in the kitchen, falling into an easy rhythm as we clear the table.

Claire dries while I rinse, her chatter filling the space like the gentle clink of dishes against porcelain.

"So, I spent my entire morning in a meeting that could have been an email," she says, huffing as she wipes a plate. "I swear to God, if I have to listen to Greg Mansell explain budget forecasting one more time, I might actually pass out at my desk."

I glance at her over my shoulder. "I thought you liked Greg."

She scoffs, but the faintest hint of pink creeps up her cheeks. "Like is a strong word. Tolerate is more accurate."

I smirk, reaching for another plate. "You're lying."

"I'm absolutely not."

"You fancy him."

Claire rolls her eyes so hard I'm surprised they don't get stuck. "I do not."

I flick water at her. "You so do."

She yelps, dodging away. "He's infuriating! He's always acting like he knows everything."

I raise an eyebrow. "And yet, you magically know exactly how he takes his coffee."

Claire points a damp dish towel at me. "First of all, that was one time. Secondly, I hate you."

I laugh, shaking my head as I set the last dish on the rack. Claire moves to the island, leaning against it, glass of wine in hand, still muttering about her boss and how he is "completely, one-hundred percent unfanciable."

My eyes drift to the envelope.

It's still sitting exactly where Dan left it, innocuous and plain. My name, just my first name and nothing else ,is written in small, careful letters.

I don't know why my stomach twists as I reach for it.

Probably because, deep down, I know it's not one of those neighborhood flyers Dan assumed it was.

Claire is still talking as I slide my finger under the flap, peeling it open.

"—and the worst part is, he keeps acting like I don't know what I'm doing, which is hilarious because I've been there longer than he has. Honestly, I don't even care that he's got nice forearms and that his voice is weirdly sexy, because..."

The words on the note stand stark against the white paper.

Do you know where your child is?

My breath catches.

For a moment, the words don't make sense. They sit there bold, unmovable, like something out of a dream, plucked from a part of my mind I don't allow myself to visit.

Then the floor tilts, the edges of the room growing too bright.

I don't realize I've dropped the note until it flutters onto the counter, the paper crumpling slightly at the edges.

Claire frowns. "Iz? You okay?"

I don't answer. My hands feel cold. My stomach tightens, my pulse hammering in my ears.

Footsteps.

Dan's voice, coming closer.

"Hey, everything okay in here?"

I can't speak.

Dan sees my face first, then follows my gaze to the note. His easy expression falters. He steps forward, brows drawing together, reaching for the paper before I can stop him.

I watch as he reads it, his jaw tightening, the muscles in his neck flexing. His grip on the note stiffens just slightly, but it's enough.

"Isabel," he says slowly, his voice measured, deliberate. "Where did this come from?"

Claire leans forward, peering at the paper over his shoulder.

"What? " She stops. I feel her mood shift instantly, the playful warmth bleeding from her tone.

"Izzy, what is this?"

My mouth is dry. The words lodge in my throat.

I don't know how to answer.

I don't know what to say.

Because I don't know what's worse. The fact that someone sent this to me or the fact that, for the briefest, most terrifying moment, I actually questioned it.

Because for one split second, before my brain caught up with reality, I really did think: *Where is Noah?*

And that kind of fear, the kind that doesn't just creep in but slams into you, the kind that digs its claws in and holds, doesn't just go away.

Even after you tell yourself it's ridiculous.

Even when you know he's safe, upstairs, sound asleep.

Because some fears don't listen to logic.

Some fears have already lived inside you for too long.

And I know, deep down, that whoever sent this, they know that, too.

4

SEVEN AND A HALF YEARS AGO

The house had ceased to feel like a stranger. Isabel now moved through its halls with ease, her footsteps measured, instinctively lighter on certain floorboards that groaned under pressure. The walls, once looming and unyielding in their silence, had softened or perhaps she had simply grown accustomed to them. The chandelier in the foyer, the towering bookshelves in the study, the scent of the house drifting through the corridors no longer felt foreign. They had become the backdrop to her days, a world unto itself, separate from the one she had known before.

Six months had passed since she arrived at Lockwood Estate, and though she still carried an awareness of her place in the house, her role, her boundaries, she had settled in. There were rhythms now, routines she could anticipate. She woke before dawn, dressed in the quiet, and made her way to the nursery before the children stirred. At eight, breakfast was served, each plate arranged identically, portions measured, glasses of milk filled to the exact same level each morning.

The children knew the routine well. Theo, always the first to wake, sat upright in his bed before Isabel even knocked on the door, blinking at her with solemn eyes that had only recently begun to hold a flicker of mischief. Charlotte, slower to rise, curled against the pillows, her small hands bunching the blankets, reluctant to abandon sleep. She had been shy at first, quiet in a way that felt unnatural for a child of three, but Isabel had noticed the subtle changes and the way she reached for Isabel's hand now, the way her giggles escaped more freely when they played.

Mornings were spent with lessons. A tutor came for Theo, an older man with neatly pressed waistcoats and an air of measured patience. Charlotte had Isabel. They practiced letters and simple sums, but mostly, they read. Charlotte loved stories, loved hearing the same ones told over and over, her tiny fingers curled into Isabel's sleeve as she listened. When lessons ended, they played outside if the weather allowed, running through the wide lawns that stretched beyond the house.

The estate had become their kingdom, a place of hidden corners and towering hedges. Isabel had learned which trees they liked to climb, where the best hiding spots were, and how Theo loved to leap from the stone steps with reckless delight while Charlotte followed cautiously, always watching before mimicking his movements. It was here, in the dappled light beneath the oak trees, that they laughed the most.

Inside, the house was different. It belonged to Evelyn and Oliver, to their sharp silences and clipped words. Isabel saw little of them. Evelyn moved like an apparition, present yet untouchable. She was beautiful in the way cold things were. She was untarnished, perfect and impossible to grasp. When she spoke to the children, it was with an air of practiced affection, brief moments of interaction that felt more like obligation than genuine warmth. She would lean down, brush a hand over Charlotte's hair, but she was already turning away before the child could react. She never raised her voice, never faltered, but Isabel had learned that silence could be just as cutting.

Oliver was more of an absence than a presence. He left before breakfast and returned after the children were asleep, his footsteps echoing in the hall long after the house had settled into its nightly hush. On the rare occasions Isabel crossed paths with him, he was always on the phone, his gaze sliding past her as though she were a shadow. She had learned not to expect acknowledgment. It was easier that way.

But the children had changed. Slowly, cautiously, as if testing the waters of something unfamiliar. At first, they had been disciplined to the point of eeriness, their movements precise and their manners impeccable. They obeyed without question, their little backs straight, their voices soft, their hands folded neatly in their laps. But now, Isabel caught glimpses of something else. Charlotte shrieked with laughter when Isabel tickled her, her tiny body collapsing into fits of giggles. Theo, once rigid in his daily structure, began pushing back in small ways, delaying bedtime by asking for just one more story, just five more minutes.

Tonight was no different. The nursery was bathed in the golden light of evening as Isabel finished tucking Charlotte into bed. The child's hair, still damp from her bath, clung to her forehead in fine curls. She blinked up sleepily, already half-lost to dreams.

Theo, however, was still wide awake.

He tugged at Isabel's sleeve, his voice a whisper. "Can we stay up late tonight?"

Isabel arched an eyebrow. "And what would we do if we did?"

Theo's lips curled into a grin. "Ghost stories."

Charlotte stirred, her voice slurred with sleep. "No," she mumbled. "Scary."

Isabel smiled, brushing a hand over Charlotte's hair. "Maybe another night," she said softly. "For now, sleep."

Theo sighed, but it was a dramatic half performance, half surrender. He pulled the blankets up to his chin, his expression wistful. Isabel reached out, smoothing the sheets, pressing a light kiss to his forehead before standing.

As she moved to the door, she hesitated, glancing back. They were watching her, both of them, their faces soft in the glow of the bedside lamp. A warmth settled in her chest unexpected and quiet.

She had not planned to love them. But she did.

The restaurant was quiet. It was the kind of place meant for discreet meetings and hushed conversations. It was old-fashioned in a deliberate way, with dark wood paneling and gilded sconces casting a warm, amber glow over the deep red upholstery. A waiter drifted past soundlessly, topping up glasses with practiced indifference. Every movement here was slow, intentional, as if the world outside did not exist.

Oliver Lockwood sat at the corner table, a space chosen for its seclusion. His posture was carefully arranged and straight-backed, hands resting lightly on either side of his untouched glass of water. He was always conscious of how he appeared to others. The appearance of control. The impression of indifference. But beneath his composed exterior, a dull pressure was building behind his ribs.

Across from him, the woman leaned forward, her fingers tight around her water glass. She spoke in low, urgent tones, her eyes flashing in the candlelight.

"You can't keep pretending this isn't happening, Oliver."

He exhaled slowly, tilting his head just slightly. "Lower your voice."

A humorless laugh escaped her lips. "You're worried about

someone hearing us?" She looked around, her gaze skimming over the other diners. No one was paying them any attention. Yet Oliver could never be sure.

"Of course you are," she added bitterly.

He didn't respond. He took a measured sip of wine. She was right, of course. Someone was always watching, even in a place like this. Especially in a place like this.

She shifted in her chair, restless, frustrated. "You always do this," she said. "Deflect. Distract. Make it about something else."

"It *is* about something else," he replied smoothly. "You think this is only about us? About what you want?"

A flicker of something crossed her face. A mix of anger, hurt and something more. She set her glass down with a deliberate *clink.*

"It *is* about me, Oliver. And it's about you." Her voice dipped lower, almost trembling. "It's about what happens next."

He leaned back slightly, shifting his weight, but he did not look away. His mind was already working through contingencies, unraveling potential fallout, considering the risks like pieces on a chessboard. He had always prided himself on being careful. Always careful.

She took a slow, controlled breath before reaching for the linen napkin folded beside her plate. Her fingers trembled only slightly as she lifted it—then, in a swift motion, slammed it onto the table. The sharp sound cut through the quiet song of conversation around them.

"I'm pregnant."

For the first time that evening, Oliver's mask slipped. His carefully constructed facade of detachment cracked for a second.

"You—" He stopped. His voice was thin, barely there.

"You need to live up to your responsibilities," she said, her voice level, but laced with something cold. "I won't be hidden away like some dirty little secret."

He said nothing and took a sip of his drink. She stood abruptly, her chair scraping against the floor. A few diners turned at the sound, but she didn't look at them. Her hands clenched into fists at her sides.

Oliver opened his mouth, but no words came.

She turned and walked out, her exit swift, final.

Oliver sat frozen, staring at the place where she had been, the scent of her perfume still hanging in the air. He swallowed hard.

He had been careful. He was always careful.

Not this time.

5

PRESENT

Dan doesn't respond right away.

He just looks at me, the note still in his hand, his fingers tightening around the edges as if he wants to crumple it. His eyes explore mine. He appears calm and steady but I catch the flicker of something deeper. Something colder.

I know that look. It's the same one he gets in court when he's deciding how to handle a situation and whether to press or back off.

Claire, on the other hand, is less subtle.

"What the hell is that supposed to mean?" she demands, glancing between us. "*Do you know where your child is?* What kind of sick joke is that?"

I force a breath, pressing my palms to the counter as if grounding myself. "It's nothing."

Claire lets out a sharp, humorless laugh. "Nothing? Izzy, that is not nothing. Someone left a creepy, cryptic message for you on your doorstep." She turns to Dan, her brows furrowing. "Are you really just going to let that slide?"

Dan speaks through gritted teeth. "No one's letting anything slide."

His voice is measured, controlled, but I can feel the weight behind it. He shifts slightly, positioning himself closer to me in an instinctive, protective gesture.

Claire isn't convinced. She turns back to me, eyes narrowing, her expression shifting from alarm to something more calculated.

"Izzy," she says slowly, carefully. "You went pale the second you read that. What's going on?"

"Nothing," I repeat too quickly.

Claire's gaze sharpens. "You're lying."

I swallow, forcing myself to hold her stare.

Claire has always been good at reading people. She notices things, the small tells, shifts in tone and changes in body language. It's part of why I liked her instantly, why I trust her.

And now, it's why she doesn't believe me.

Before she can push further, Dan steps in.

"Izzy doesn't need to justify some random piece of paper, Claire," he says evenly. "It's probably just some stupid prank."

Claire blinks at him, then gestures toward the note. "A prank? This doesn't feel like a prank, Dan. It feels personal."

I see the way her mind is working, how she's trying to connect dots that aren't there, or at least, not in the way she thinks.

She doesn't know.

She has no idea about the Lockwood children. About that night. About the storm of headlines, the whispers, the way people used to look at me before I disappeared from that world.

She knows nothing about Carrie.

And Dan knows everything.

He knew when he married me. When I sat him down and told him, hands shaking, waiting for him to look at me the way everyone else had. But he didn't. He listened, then reached across the space between us, took my hand, and said, *I believe you.*

For the first time in years, I felt like I could breathe.

And now, he's doing it again.

"I'll call the neighborhood watch," Dan says smoothly, placing the note down as if it's nothing more than an inconvenience. "Maybe someone's had something similar. Could be kids messing around."

Claire doesn't look convinced. She crosses her arms, lips pursed, still watching me too closely.

I exhale slowly, forcing a smile. "Dan's right. It's probably nothing."

Claire studies me for a long moment, her eyes flicking between my face and the note.

"Fine," she says eventually, but I don't miss the way her voice is clipped or how she doesn't look away immediately.

Instead, she presses her lips together and picks up her glass, draining the last of her wine.

Dan reaches for my hand under the counter, giving it a small squeeze. I squeeze back.

I know he's trying to reassure me. And for a moment, I almost let it work. Almost. But the note still sits between us, untouched, its meaning curling in the air like smoke. And no matter how much I want to believe it's nothing, I already know it's not.

~

The weekend rolls in slow and easy, carrying with it the kind of crisp autumn air that seeps through window cracks, making everything feel sharper, more in focus.

Dan offers to take Noah to the park for the morning, giving

me some time to myself, and before I know it, I'm in the car, heading toward Claire's apartment.

Her place is nothing like mine.

She lives in a neat, modern space on the top floor of a small complex just outside of town. It's the kind of apartment with large, spotless windows that let in just the right amount of light, where the furniture is sleek and minimal, and not a single thing is out of place.

It strikes me every time I come here how orderly it all is. How unlike Claire it feels.

Claire, who always spills wine when she talks too much with her hands. Claire, who tosses her coat over whatever chair is closest. Claire, who leaves a trail of chaos wherever she goes. And yet, here in her apartment, nothing is out of place.

It makes me wonder if this is who she really is when no one's watching.

She opens the door before I even knock. "Izzy! Get in here. You look like you need coffee, or possibly something stronger."

I laugh, stepping inside as she closes the door behind me. "It's barely noon."

She waves a hand. "There's no time restriction on mimosas."

I shake my head, kicking off my shoes as she moves into the kitchen. She's wearing a soft cream sweater, her blonde curls pinned up lazily, and for a moment, she looks as relaxed as ever. Like nothing is wrong.

But something is wrong.

The envelope. The note.

It's been two days, and I still can't shake the feeling that someone is watching me.

"Alright," Claire says, setting down two mugs and sliding into the chair across from me. "What's new?"

I force a smile. "Not much. Dan's had a busy week, Noah is in a dinosaur phase again, and I,"

Claire tilts her head, waiting as I clear my throat and reach for my coffee. "I've just been keeping busy."

She watches me for a second, then sighs. "Izzy."

I brace myself.

She leans forward, resting her elbows on the table. "The note."

I swallow, pretending to focus on my drink. "What about it?"

Claire raises an eyebrow. "Are we seriously going to pretend that wasn't weird as hell?"

I exhale, setting my mug down. "It was weird. But it was probably just a prank, like Dan said."

She doesn't look convinced. "You didn't seem like you thought it was a prank."

"Because it freaked me out," I admit. "But nothing else has happened. No more notes, no creepy phone calls, no one lurking outside my house. It was a one off."

Claire tilts her head, studying me. "Has anything like that ever happened before?"

The question is light, casual. But there's something in her tone which is careful and measured.

I force myself to shake my head. "No."

Lie.

But Claire doesn't push. Instead, she reaches across the table, resting her hand lightly over mine.

"You've been through so much, haven't you?"

Her voice is soft, understanding, and for a second, something in me wavers.

I could tell her.

I could tell her about the past. I could tell her about the headlines, about the children who drowned, about the woman who watched my life unravel with cold satisfaction. I could tell her about the things people said about me, about the whispers I still hear in my head when the nights get too quiet.

But I don't. Because some things are better left buried.

Instead, I nod slightly. "Yeah."

Claire squeezes my hand gently before pulling back, offering a small smile. "Well, if it happens again, you tell me, okay?"

I nod again, my stomach twisting.

Because I already know this isn't over.

Claire doesn't push any further about the note. Instead, she leans back in her chair, stretching her arms above her head before reaching for her coffee again.

"You know what we need?" she says, drumming her nails against the side of the mug.

I glance at her, forcing myself to stay in the moment. "A million dollars and a time machine?"

She snorts. "Close. A vacation."

I blink, caught off guard. "A vacation?"

"Yes." She sits up straighter, eyes bright. "Somewhere warm. Somewhere with bottomless cocktails and cabana boys who bring you snacks without you even having to ask." She grins, waggling her eyebrows. "A cruise, actually. I've been thinking about it for a while."

I attempt a smile, but my mind feels distant, preoccupied with something else that feels heavier.

"Oh yeah?" I ask, trying to sound interested, though my chest is still tight.

She nods. "Yeah! I've been looking at this one that goes around the Caribbean. Sun, sea, ridiculous amounts of food. What more could a girl want?"

Claire is fully in her element now, painting the scene like she's already there. She talks with her hands, and I watch her nails flash as she gestures animatedly. I want to get swept up in her enthusiasm, to let myself imagine the warm sand underfoot, the weightlessness of floating in the ocean, the sun pressing down on my shoulders like a warm hand.

But my brain won't let me.

Because all I can think about is the note.

The way it sat on my counter, waiting for me to read it.

The way my heart nearly stopped when I saw the words: *Do you know where your child is?*

The memory grips me like a fist, and I force myself to push it away. Claire doesn't notice. She's still talking, oblivious to the fact that I'm miles away.

"And you should come with me," she says suddenly, her voice slicing through my thoughts.

I blink. "What?"

She grins, reaching for my hand and giving it a squeeze. "Think about it, Izzy. You and me, cocktails in hand, lounging in the sun with no responsibilities. No laundry, no meal planning, no *Mommy, where's my dinosaur?* every five seconds."

I let out a small laugh, because the idea of a real break is tempting. But before I can even let myself entertain the thought, my instincts kick in.

I shake my head. "I can't."

Claire groans, flopping back against her chair. "Why not?"

"Because I have a family," I say, still half-smiling, as if that explains everything.

She waves a hand. "Families survive when moms take vacations, you know. It's actually a thing that happens."

I smirk, but I already know I'm not budging. "Claire."

She sits up, leaning forward. "No, seriously. Why not?"

I hesitate, feeling the words tangle in my throat.

Because the idea of leaving them makes something twist uncomfortably in my chest.

Because I know what it's like to have everything ripped away in a single moment. Because I know what it's like to be blamed for it. Because if something happened while I was gone, I wouldn't survive it.

"I just... I wouldn't enjoy myself, knowing I left them behind," I say instead, keeping my voice light.

Claire watches me carefully. "Izzy, when was the last time you did something just for you?"

I glance down at my coffee, shifting uncomfortably. "I do things for myself."

"Like what?"

I open my mouth, then shut it again.

She smirks. "Exactly."

I frown. "That's not true. I take time for myself."

Claire raises an eyebrow. "Taking a shower without being interrupted by a three-year-old doesn't count."

I exhale, shaking my head, but she's not letting it go.

"When was the last time you had an actual break?" she presses. "A real one, where you weren't thinking about Noah, or Dan, or what needs to be done next?"

I don't answer. Because the truth is, I can't remember.

Claire softens, her voice dropping just a little. "You deserve to be a person too, Izzy."

I swallow, gripping my mug tightly. "I am a person."

She tilts her head, giving me a look that makes something squirm inside me. "Are you?"

Something about the question makes my stomach knot.

Claire doesn't mean anything by it. I know that. She just wants me to say yes, to shrug it off, to let her book the cruise and pretend for a moment that life is as simple as choosing to let go.

But I can't let go. I haven't been able to let go for years.

So instead, I force a smile and say, "I just can't."

Claire studies me for a long moment, then sighs, holding up her hands. "Alright, alright. I'll drop it. But if you change your mind..."

"I won't."

She smirks. "We'll see."

I try to match her lightheartedness, but something in me is still coiled too tight.

Because no matter how much I want to pretend everything is fine, I know that something is coming. And I can feel it getting closer.

6

SEVEN AND A HALF YEARS AGO

The house glowed like a lantern in the dark, its enormous windows spilling warm, golden light onto the front drive, where sleek cars idled and chauffeurs stood like sentinels. Through the long, arched windows, a glittering spectacle unfolded in a room thick with self-satisfied laughter, the clink of expensive crystal, and the smooth hum of conversation that never dipped below absolute ease.

Evelyn Lockwood was in her element. She moved through the gilded haze of the dining hall like a lithe cat, self-possessed, entirely unbothered by the very event that bore her name. This was her stage, and she played the part effortlessly. A hostess in the truest sense, she never lingered too long with any one guest, instead bestowing attention like a benevolent queen, making each person feel, if only for a moment, as though they were the most important in the room.

The occasion was their seventh wedding anniversary, a fact Evelyn had permitted to be mentioned but not dwelled upon. There were more pressing things to celebrate and connections to forge, hands to shake, impressions to solidify. Marriage, after all, was only part of the equation.

Oliver, on the other hand, played his role with markedly less enthusiasm. He wore the expression of a man dutifully present, neither engaged nor entirely absent, exerting charm only where required. He lingered in conversation with men of consequence, politicians, business magnates and the kind of men he might need something from one day. To everyone else, he was pleasant, agreeable, but never wholly there.

The dining room was a masterpiece of restrained opulence. French doors flung open to the terrace, a hundred candles flickering in glass hurricane lanterns set at careful intervals along the long mahogany table. The air was thick with the scent of roasted meat and herbs, wine poured in a silent, endless stream by uniformed waitstaff who moved with the soft efficiency of ghosts. Outside, beyond the manicured lawn, the ocean stretched unseen in the dark.

A waiter passed with a silver tray gliding at shoulder height, as Evelyn plucked a champagne flute without breaking stride. She caught Oliver's eye across the room and smiled. It was not a warm, familiar smile, but something curated, a performance for their audience. He did not return it. Instead, he lifted his own glass to his lips, his gaze dropping before their guests could read too much into the moment.

She reached him eventually, her approach seamless, all the calculated choreography of a seasoned hostess. When she spoke, it was in that hushed, clipped tone meant only for him.

"You might at least pretend to enjoy yourself."

Oliver's mouth curled slightly, though not into anything resembling amusement. "I am enjoying myself."

"You're fooling no one."

"No, that's what you're doing, as effortlessly as always."

Her smile remained fixed, but the light in her eyes sharpened. "If you're going to sulk through the evening, do it somewhere discreet."

He gave a humorless laugh. “I think we’ve passed discretion.”

Evelyn placed her fingers lightly on his wrist, a gesture so casual, so natural, that an observer might mistake it for affection. But Oliver felt the subtle pressure there, the hint of steel beneath the softness.

“Smile,” she murmured, lifting her glass to her lips. “It’s our anniversary.”

From somewhere beyond the grand dining room, the muffled laughter of children echoed down the hall, distant but unmistakable. Isabel had been tucked away with them for the evening, ushered into the far reaches of the house where her presence would not interfere with the evening’s elegance. Evelyn had not needed to explain this arrangement to her. She understood the rules by now.

The guests were beautiful, sharp-eyed, and well-dressed, their conversations laced with the effortless cruelty of people who had never known the dull weight of consequence. A woman in a shimmering navy gown trailed her fingers idly along the rim of her wine glass as she spoke, her voice lilting with amusement. “Oh, but Evelyn, how do you do it? Everything looks so effortless.”

“Because it is,” Evelyn returned smoothly, her tone just warm enough to make it impossible to determine whether she was joking.

The woman laughed, leaning in. “Truly, I don’t know how you put up with it,” She gestured vaguely toward Oliver. “Marriage, I mean.”

Oliver glanced up from his drink, a small flicker of something sharp passing through his gaze. Evelyn smiled, again, a careful, curated thing. “You make allowances,” she said light, turning her attention back to the room at large.

The night carried on, golden and indulgent, a portrait of

effortless affluence. And yet, beneath the polish, something unseen stirred, lurking just beyond the candlelit perfection.

The long dining table was a vision of opulence. Over twenty guests sat poised, their conversation flowing like the wine in their glasses, tinged with the vague satisfaction of people who had never known hunger, true misfortune, or anything outside the bubble of their own refinement. The clink of cutlery, the low ripple of laughter. It was a well-oiled symphony of indulgence.

At the head of the table, Evelyn Lockwood rose to her feet, a slow and deliberate motion that caused the chatter to dwindle. She was radiant, her champagne-colored gown catching the candlelight, her expression unreadable except for the faintest curl of amusement at the corner of her mouth. She lifted her glass and exhaled, as if she had been waiting for this moment all evening.

“My dear friends,” she began, her voice smooth as silk, “what a joy it is to have you all here tonight, celebrating what can only be described as a milestone—seven years of marriage.” A few polite chuckles rippled through the crowd. Evelyn allowed herself a knowing smile before continuing. “Marriage is a curious thing, isn’t it? A dance, a negotiation. It demands patience, grace, and above all, honesty.”

Oliver, seated beside her, shifted slightly in his chair. He tilted his glass toward his lips but did not drink. A flicker of movement at the far end of the table and Carrie, his secretary. Her pale face was fixed on that of her hostess.

Evelyn’s gaze swept the table with practiced ease, her amusement growing. “Of course, one cannot always expect honesty in return.”

The room stilled. A guest coughed lightly into his napkin, the sound swallowed by the thick silence settling over the table.

"Fortunately, I have always believed in the importance of transparency," Evelyn continued, her voice lilting, almost playful. "And I was fortunate enough to have a dear friend dining in the city just the other evening. Imagine my surprise when she called to say she had witnessed the most dramatic little scene at one of our favorite restaurants." She turned her head slightly, her eyes landing on Carrie, whose breath caught audibly. "A young woman storming out, devastated. A man sitting alone, stunned."

Carrie's chair scraped softly against the floor. Her face had gone ghostly white.

Evelyn tilted her head, feigning curiosity. "Now, my dear, why don't you introduce yourself to the guests? Since you are already so well-acquainted with my husband, I think it only fair that everyone here knows who you are."

A suffocating pause fell over the table. Someone set their glass down too forcefully, the sound shattering the quiet. Carrie's lips parted, her breath ragged. The color had drained completely from her face.

“I—” she stammered, her voice failing her.

"Oh, come now, Carrie," Evelyn pressed, her tone honeyed, but her eyes sharp as a blade. "You weren't so shy when you were sneaking off to lunch with Oliver. Your boss."

A murmur rippled through the guests. Low, scandalized, hungry.

Carrie swallowed hard, her hands trembling as she pushed back her chair with a sudden, jerky motion. “Excuse me,” she whispered, barely audible, and then she was fleeing through the great hall, leaving a table of guests whose mouths hung open like fish on a line.

Oliver watched her go but did not move. Instead, he let the silence stretch just long enough to make everyone uncomfortable before exhaling and leaning back in his chair. "Well," he said lazily, taking a sip of his drink. "That's what I get for dipping my pen in the office ink."

A sharp, masculine laugh rang out from the far end of the table, quickly stifled. Evelyn arched a brow, unfazed, then tilted her glass toward Oliver. "And yet, here we are," she mused. "Seven years. Can you imagine?"

Oliver exhaled, shaking his head, and then, without another word, pushed back his chair and stood. He straightened his jacket, nodded once toward their stunned guests, and made his exit with the same detachment as a man leaving an uninteresting business meeting. The room remained painfully silent until the heavy study door clicked shut behind him.

Evelyn, still standing, let the moment settle before turning back to the guests with the most effortless of smiles. "Now, let's enjoy this wonderful meal," she said pleasantly. "The chef has outdone himself tonight."

The tension at the table was thick enough to carve, but the waitstaff resumed their duties without hesitation, moving between the guests as if the scandal had never occurred. The knives and forks resumed their gentle clinking, and conversation picked up in nervous spurts. Evelyn, for her part, simply smiled, satisfied.

Outside, in the cool of the night, Carrie disappeared into the dark, her sobs swallowed by the wind. And inside, behind the closed doors of his study, Oliver poured himself another drink, settling into the quiet like a man who had already decided the night was over for him.

7

PRESENT

The bags are heavier than I expected.

I set them down on the kitchen island with a sigh, rolling my shoulders back as I glance at the clock. It's barely past noon, but I already feel like I've lived a full day.

Noah stomps past me, making sure I hear every deliberate footstep.

I pretend not to notice.

I know better than to feed the storm while it's still gathering, swirling inside his small, stubborn frame. He's sulking, his lower lip jutted out, arms crossed, a dark cloud hanging over him like a cartoon character with a storm hovering over their head.

I exhale slowly and turn back to the bags.

The kitchen is bathed in cool, late-morning light spilling through the large window above the sink. It should feel warm and comforting, the kind of place that invites you to linger over a cup of coffee, but today, everything feels off-kilter. The air is thick, almost charged, like the house itself is holding its breath.

The faint smell of citrus and fresh bread are drifting from the open bags. But underneath it all, there's something else. It the steady, rhythmic sound of plastic wheels grinding against the floor.

Noah lies flat on his stomach in the middle of the room, one cheek pressed against the tiles, his fingers gripping a small red car. He pushes it forward, then pulls it back. Again. And again. And again.

The sound grates, catching on the raw edges of my nerves.

I pull a carton of eggs from one of the bags and place it carefully in the fridge, pressing my lips together.

I know this game.

He wanted to go to the swings. I told him we needed to take the groceries home first. Now, I am the worst mother in the world.

A bag of apples. A block of cheese. A pack of pasta.

The car scrapes back. The car scrapes forward.

I clench my jaw, willing myself to breathe through it.

He's tired. He's three. It's not personal.

Still, the noise digs under my skin, relentless and steady, like a slow drip from a leaking faucet.

I catch my reflection in the darkened oven door as I reach for a pack of chicken. I look exactly how I feel rumpled, drained, frayed at the edges. My hair is pulled into a loose bun, tendrils slipping free at my temples. My sweater is soft but slightly stretched, my jeans snug at the waist. The shadows under my eyes are faint but present, a whisper of exhaustion that never fully fades.

The car grinds again, louder this time.

My fingers tighten around the carton of milk.

"Noah," I say, keeping my voice even, soft. "Can you play in the living room, sweetheart?"

He doesn't look up. "No."

The response is instant, sharp in its defiance.

I press my tongue against the roof of my mouth, forcing patience.

"It's just... Mommy's trying to concentrate, and that sound is very loud in here."

He says nothing. The car keeps moving.

I exhale and turn back to the bags, my fingers trembling slightly as I grab a loaf of bread.

This isn't about the car. This isn't even about the swings. This is about control.

He doesn't have it. So now, he's trying to take it, one slow, deliberate scrape at a time. I understand it, even as it unravels me.

The last of the groceries go into the cupboards with a little more force than necessary. I press my hands against the counter, staring out the window, trying to breathe through the tightness in my chest.

Outside, the street is quiet. A bird flutters onto the porch railing, tilts its head, then darts away. A woman in yoga pants walks briskly past the house, earbuds in, ponytail swaying.

Normal. Everything looks so normal. Except it isn't.

The note from two days ago still lingers at the edge of my thoughts, ghosting over my skin like a draft from an open window.

Do you know where your child is?

The words slip into my mind unwelcome and intrusive.

I squeeze my eyes shut for a moment, pressing my fingertips into the counter.

The car scrapes. Back. Forth. Louder.

I whip around before I can stop myself. "Noah."

He stops.

Looks up at me.

His big brown eyes are wide, expectant. Testing.

I force a slow breath through my nose and soften my voice. "Do you want to help me put away the snacks?"

A beat of silence.

Then, reluctantly, he pushes himself up, leaving the car abandoned on the floor.

He doesn't say anything, but he drags himself over to the counter, watching as I pull out a box of animal crackers.

"Here," I say, handing it to him.

He hesitates, then takes it. His fingers curl around the box, holding it like a peace offering.

The tension in my chest loosens. A little.

I reach out, smoothing my hand over the top of his head. His curls are warm, messy, sticking to his forehead.

"I know you really wanted to go to the swings," I say softly. "We'll go later, okay?"

His shoulders relax just slightly. He gives a small nod and opens the cupboard where his snacks go.

I turn back to the counter, and rub my hands over my face. The moment has passed. But I still feel off-balance, like something is shifting just beyond my line of sight.

The note. The feeling I can't shake.

Noah wanders off, his small feet padding across the hardwood as he drags his red car behind him. I hear him settle in the entrance porch, the familiar plastic rattle of wheels against wood beginning again—this time slower, more deliberate.

I let out a quiet breath and roll my shoulders back. The house is peaceful now—or at least carries a stillness that feels close enough.

The last of the shopping is put away, the cupboard doors closing with soft clicks. I wipe my hands on a dish towel, glancing around the kitchen to make sure everything is back where it should be.

I don't hear the sound at first. A faint rustle. The soft whump of paper landing on wood.

Noah hears it, though.

Lying flat on his stomach, car clutched in his little hand, he watches with curiosity as something thin and white flutters through the letterbox, gliding silently to the floor beside him.

He blinks at it. Then he glances toward the kitchen.

I don't come.

His annoyance about the swings is already forgotten.

Noah reaches out, fingers curling around the paper. It's just a normal envelope, the same kind he's seen before when mail drops through the door. It doesn't occur to him to tell me about it. Instead, he decides it's the perfect thing to build a tunnel.

He presses it against the floor, curving it into a small arch, balancing it carefully so his car can zoom underneath. He grins, making sound effects as he pushes the car back and forth, watching it disappear into the paper tunnel before reappearing on the other side. For the next few minutes, he's completely absorbed.

Blissfully unaware. And in the kitchen, so am I.

I run a damp cloth over the counter, fold the shopping bags neatly, and glance at my phone. I exhale, pressing my hands against my lower back. The day is slipping by, and I know I need to keep my promise.

I head toward the entrance porch, my socked feet quiet against the wood.

"Alright, kiddo," I say lightly, "now we can go to the swings."

Noah doesn't answer right away. He's still lying on the floor, face inches from the ground, watching as his car coasts smoothly under the arch. It's only when I get closer that I see it properly.

The envelope. My name on the front. Not typed. Not printed. Carefully handwritten in neat, slanted letters.

My breath catches and I snatch it up before I even think, my stomach twisting.

"Noah." My voice is sharp. Too sharp. "Where did you get this?"

He startles slightly, rolling onto his side to look up at me. His brown eyes are wide, uncertain.

"It came through the door," he says, like it's obvious. "I made a tunnel."

I stare at him, my heart slamming too fast in my chest. "Did you see who put it there?"

He shakes his head. "No."

My fingers tighten around the envelope. I glance toward the door, half expecting to see someone standing there, watching through the glass. But the porch is empty. The street beyond it is still.

Noah shifts on the floor, uneasy.

"Mommy?" His voice is smaller now. "What's wrong?"

I snap back to him, realizing how I must look, rigid, tense, fingers white-knuckled around the paper.

I force my grip to loosen. I swallow, shaking my head, trying to smooth out the sharp edge in my voice.

"Nothing, sweetheart," I say, softer this time. "It's just... just a surprise, that's all."

He watches me, his little brow furrowed, his hands now gripping his car like an anchor.

I hate that I've made him feel like this. That my fear has bled into him.

I smooth my expression, kneeling beside him. "Hey," I say gently, brushing his curls away from his forehead. "It's okay. I was just—just caught off guard."

He hesitates. "You looked scared."

I smile, even though it feels thin. "I was just surprised. That's all."

He watches me for a second longer, then nods, slowly accepting my words.

I press a quick kiss to the top of his head. "Go get your shoes, buddy. We'll go to the swings now."

His face brightens, his worry dissolving as quickly as it arrived. He scrambles up, abandoning his car and running toward the hallway.

I watch him go, my hands still trembling. Then, I look down at the envelope. And finally, I open it.

The envelope trembles in my hands. I can feel my pulse behind my eyes, in my throat, in the tips of my fingers as I unfold the paper and read the message written inside.

He is mine.

The words are inked in the same careful, deliberate handwriting as before. Each letter precise, controlled, as if the person writing them wasn't rushed. As if they enjoyed taking their time.

A cold weight presses against my chest. For a moment, all I can hear is the tick of the kitchen clock. Then, from down the hall, the sound of Noah rummaging for his shoes. I squeeze my eyes shut.

Think, Izzy.

When I open them, I move on instinct.

I fold the note, slip it into my pocket, and take a deep breath before calling out—steady, even, controlled.

"Noah?"

His small voice echoes back, muffled from the closet. "I can't find my blue shoes!"

I force a smile into my voice. "That's okay, sweetheart. Come here for a second."

There's a pause, then the patter of his feet against the floor. He appears in the hallway, his curls slightly mussed from digging through the shoe bin.

His little face is expectant. Hopeful.

"Are we going?"

I hate this. I hate what I have to say next.

I crouch down, tucking a loose curl behind his ear. "Actually, buddy... change of plan."

His face crumples immediately. "What? But you said—"

"I know." My voice stays soft, but my hands are shaking. "But I just remembered something really important I need to do first."

His lip juts out, frustration rolling back in. "But you said we could go when the shopping was done."

I nod, my throat tightening. "I know I did. But I promise we'll go later, okay? Maybe after dinner."

He doesn't like this answer. His brows pinch together, frustration bubbling in his little chest, and I can see the storm gathering again.

I don't have time for it.

I push myself up, ruffling his hair like I would on any other normal day. "Why don't you go pick out a movie to watch? I'll make popcorn."

He huffs, crossing his arms. "I don't want a movie."

I grab the front door key, twisting the lock firmly.

Click.

A sound so final it makes my stomach lurch.

Noah watches me with a frown. "Why are you locking the door?"

I force another smile. "Just because."

It's a weak answer, but it's all I can manage. Because what am I supposed to say? Because someone is watching. Because someone thinks you belong to them. Because I don't know what I'll do if I lose you.

Instead, I turn, moving quickly through the house. Checking the locks on the back door. Sliding my hands over the window frames, making sure they're shut. Moving upstairs, pulling down latches, double-checking every point of entry.

With each lock I secure, my breath comes a little faster, my skin prickling with cold despite the warmth of the house.

Noah trails behind me at first, watching with confusion. But as I move from room to room, his excitement fades into something else. Something uneasy.

He tugs at my sleeve. "Mommy?"

I turn, crouching in front of him. I need to fix this. I need to fix my face. I smooth my expression, soften my voice. "Hmm?"

His little fingers twist in the hem of my sweater. "Why are you locking everything?"

I cup his cheek, brushing my thumb over his skin. "Just making sure everything is safe."

His brows furrow. "But it's already safe."

I nod. "It is. But it's my job to double-check, okay?"

He hesitates, searching my face, trying to decide whether he believes me. Finally, he nods.

I kiss his forehead again. "Go pick a movie."

He shuffles off, slower this time, pausing to glance back at me before disappearing into the living room.

I let out a slow breath. Then, I grab my phone.

Dan answers on the second ring.

"Hey, you. What's up?" His voice is warm, easy. Unaware.

I swallow, pressing a hand to my stomach. "I need you to come home."

There's a pause. A small shift in his tone. "Izzy?"

I close my eyes. "Please."

He doesn't hesitate. "I'm on my way."

8

PRESENT

I wake up with a gasp.

The kind that rips through your throat, sharp and panicked, like you've surfaced too fast from deep water.

The room is dark, but my heart is hammering, my breath caught somewhere between a dream and something worse. I don't remember what I was dreaming about, only that it left something clawing at my ribs, something cold curling around my spine.

Something is wrong.

The air feels different. The stillness is off.

I sit up too fast, my pulse a frantic drumbeat in my ears.

Dan stirs beside me, mumbling something incoherent, half-dragged from sleep.

I don't answer. I'm already sliding out of bed, my bare feet meeting the cool wood floor.

There's a sound so faint I almost don't hear it. A whisper of air. A shift in space.

It's coming from the hallway.

I freeze, every muscle tensing. My body screams at me to move, to run, but I force myself to listen first.

Nothing.

Only silence.

But *I know. I know* someone was here.

My skin prickles as I step toward the door, breath shallow, fingers clutching the edge of the frame. I peer into the darkness beyond, every nerve in my body wound so tight I feel like I might snap.

The hallway is empty. The house is silent. But it wasn't. Not before.

I turn qucikly, my voice breaking the quiet.

"Dan?"

He groans, shifting onto his back. "Mmm?"

I don't have time for his sluggishness. My breath comes too fast, my chest too tight. So I grab his arm, shaking him hard. "Dan. Someone was in the house."

That wakes him up.

His eyes snap open, squinting in the darkness as he pushes himself up on his elbows. "What?"

I swallow. "Someone was here."

He blinks, still groggy. "Izzy—"

"I heard something," I say, my voice too high, too sharp. "The air felt different. Like it moved. Someone was in here, Dan."

He rubs a hand over his face, sighing. "Izzy..."

I don't wait for him to finish whatever rationalization is sitting on his tongue. I'm already moving.

I push open the bedroom door and step into the hallway. The floor creaks under my weight, the sound too loud in the suffocating quiet of the house.

Dan follows, his bare feet lighter against the floorboards as he catches up. "Izzy, slow down."

I ignore him. My stomach is in knots, my heart rattling against my ribs.

I reach the entrance hall and stop dead. The front door is unlocked.

My breath catches, my arms prickling with cold.

"Dan." I point.

He exhales, stepping past me, his hand closing over the handle. "I must've forgotten to lock it."

"No." The word is out before I can stop it, fierce and desperate.

He looks at me.

"I locked it." My voice shakes. "I know I did."

He hesitates, his brows knitting together, then lets out a slow breath. "Maybe I unlocked it when I let the dog out or something"

I put my hand on my hip. "We don't have a dog, Dan."

He rubs a hand over his jaw, exhaling through his nose. "Okay. Then maybe I just thought I locked it before bed."

I shake my head, the air pressing in too tight.

"Someone was in here."

"Izzy." His voice is firmer now, more awake. "Look at me."

I don't. My eyes stay fixed on the door, my mind racing. I locked it. I know I did.

Dan sighs, stepping in front of me, blocking my view. His hands land gently on my shoulders. "Noah's here. We're here. Nothing happened."

I shake my head again, but it's weaker this time. My limbs feel unsteady, my breath too fast, too sharp.

"We should call the police," I whisper.

Dan hesitates.

"Izzy..."

"What if someone's watching?" My voice is barely above a breath now.

Dan closes his eyes for a brief second, as if gathering

patience. When he opens them again, his grip on my arms tightens slightly.

"The past is in the past," he says carefully. "Nothing is going to happen to Noah."

I flinch.

Not because of his words, but because I don't believe them.

Because I can't. Because I've learned that the past never really stays buried.

Dan exhales, softening. He tucks a strand of hair behind my ear, his fingers brushing my cheek. "Come back to bed, okay? We'll double-check everything in the morning."

I waver, caught between the weight in my chest and the exhaustion creeping into my bones.

Finally, I nod.

But as Dan locks the door and leads me back upstairs, I can't shake the feeling that I'm walking away from something I shouldn't ignore.

Something waiting. Something just out of sight.

The voices downstairs pull me from sleep before I fully realize where I am.

For a second, I lie still, my mind thick with exhaustion, my limbs heavy. The covers are too warm, the house too quiet except for the low murmur of conversation drifting up from the kitchen.

Dan called her.

I know it before I even get out of bed.

I push the blankets back, rubbing a hand over my face as I sit up. My head feels sluggish, fogged with the weight of a restless night. I barely remember drifting off—only that I kept jolting awake, staring at the ceiling, listening for sounds that weren't there.

But something had been there.

Someone had been in the house.

I take a deep breath, forcing my nerves to settle before making my way downstairs.

The moment I step into the kitchen, Claire turns, her sharp blue eyes locking onto me.

"Morning, Sleeping Beauty."

Her tone is light, but I see the tension coiled in her shoulders, the way her fingers tighten around her coffee mug. Dan stands by the counter, arms folded, his face unreadable.

I don't smile.

Claire exhales, setting her cup down. "So, Dan filled me in."

I shoot him a look. "Seriously?"

Dan doesn't flinch. "Yes, seriously." He gestures toward Claire. "You wouldn't talk to me. Maybe you'll talk to her."

"I have talked to you," I mutter, moving toward the coffee machine. My hands shake slightly as I reach for a mug.

"You've avoided me," he corrects, his voice calm but firm.

I clench my jaw, pouring my coffee. "I'm fine."

Claire lets out a sharp, disbelieving laugh. "Oh yeah, you're totally fine. That's why you nearly ripped the front door off last night, thinking a murderer was in your living room."

I slam the coffee pot down harder than necessary.

She sighs, her voice softening. "Izzy, look. I get it. This whole thing is creepy as hell. But Noah is safe. You are safe. And if some lunatic is messing with you, we need to figure out who."

I swallow, gripping my coffee mug tightly.

Dan exhales and picks something up from the counter. An envelope. My stomach clenches. I already know which one it is before he holds it up.

Claire's gazes at it, her brows pulling together. "That the note?"

Dan nods and hands it to her.

She takes it carefully, her expression shifting from curiosity to something darker as she unfolds the paper and reads the words inside.

He is mine.

The color drains from her face.

She looks up sharply, first at me, then at Dan. "What the fuck?"

Dan leans against the counter, rubbing a hand over his jaw. "Yeah."

Claire's mouth opens, then shuts again as she stares at the note. She reads it once more, slower this time, as if trying to decipher some hidden meaning. Then, suddenly, she pushes back her chair and stands.

"Alright," she says, tossing the note onto the table. "We're calling the police."

"No." My response is instant, automatic.

Claire's eyes snap to mine. "Izzy."

"I said no."

Claire blinks, then lets out a slow breath, dragging a hand through her hair. "Okay. Fine. Let's just take a second here." She turns to Dan. "And you? You're okay with just sitting on this?"

Dan hesitates, looking between us. "I don't think it's that simple."

Claire's brows shoot up. "It's exactly that simple. Someone is leaving these notes at your house. Someone is trying to mess with Izzy." Her expression hardens. "We don't know what they're capable of."

I exhale loudly. "We don't even know who 'they' are."

"Then let's find out."

She says it so easily, like it's something that can be solved in an afternoon. Like we can put a name and a face to the fear curling in my gut.

But we can't.

Because whoever is doing this, whoever is watching, knows me. Knows my son. And knows exactly what to say to get inside my head.

Claire crosses her arms. "Fine. If you don't want to call the police, tell me this. Who do you think it is?"

Silence.

I stare down into my coffee, my grip tightening around the mug.

Claire huffs. "Izzy."

I look up at her.

She shakes her head. "Come on. You don't get notes like this at random. This isn't some kid pulling a prank. Someone knows exactly what they're doing."

Dan shifts slightly. "Claire—"

"No, Dan." She holds up the note. "This is messed up. Someone is trying to scare her. And it's working." She turns back to me. "So tell me. Who the hell would want to do this?"

The room feels too small. Too bright.

I swallow, forcing myself to sound steady. "I don't know."

Claire's gaze pierces into me, searching my face. She doesn't believe me.

I don't blame her. But I can't say it. I can't say her name. I can't give voice to the possibility pressing against the edges of my mind.

Because if I say it out loud, it makes it real.

I don't let myself finish the thought.

Instead, I take a slow breath and set my coffee down, pressing my palms against the table as I meet Claire's stare.

"No police," I say again, quieter this time.

Claire clenches her jaw, then lets out a puff of air from her mouth, shaking her head. "Fine."

But the look in her eyes says this isn't over. Not even close.

9

SEVEN AND A HALF YEARS AGO

The apartment stank of sweat, iron, and something deeper. Something stale and coppery that clung to the heavy fabric of the sheets, to the walls, to the air itself. Two days had passed, or maybe longer, since she had last moved from the bed. The bloodied sheets beneath her had dried stiff, the stains blooming like rusted flowers across the fabric.

Carrie sat hunched in the center of it all, knees drawn to her chest, arms wrapped around them, her body curled inward like something abandoned, forgotten. Her nightdress, once pale blue, was darkened in places, clinging damply to her skin. She rocked back and forth, slow and rhythmic, the way a mother might soothe a colicky child, except there was no child now.

The curtains were drawn, but the city beyond the thin walls throbbed dully, headlights washing in thin ribbons beneath the fabric, indifferent. The radiator in the corner ticked softly, a metronome to the cavernous silence of the room. Her breath came shallow, nearly imperceptible, her lips dry and cracked from days of dehydration.

She had not screamed when it happened. Had not gasped, wept, or called anyone. The pain had been sharp, splitting her open from the inside, but she had known, perhaps even before the first cramps, that this was always how it would end. A body under too much stress. A baby that was never meant to be. The blood had come in a rush, hot and violent, and she had merely watched it spread beneath her, pooling against the mattress, a quiet, inevitable tide.

Oliver had not called. Not once.

The thought floated to the surface like a dead fish, belly-up. She should have expected it, but still, it gnawed at her. He had never promised anything. No illusions, no whispers of love, nothing beyond the cold, hard fact of what they were to each other. But she had thought, somewhere deep in the quiet, foolish part of herself, that he would care. At least enough to check.

She let her head drop to her knees. Her arms tightened around her shins, fingers digging into her flesh until it hurt. She wanted to dissolve into the mattress, to sink into the filth she had created and disappear. The stench of old blood had become part of her, seeping into her pores, thick and cloying.

The phone sat on the nightstand. It hadn't rung in days.

A dull knock sounded at the door. Not Oliver. He wouldn't come.

She did not move. Did not breathe.

Another knock, hesitant. Then silence.

A moment later, the sound of footsteps retreating down the hall.

She exhaled, long and shuddering, and closed her eyes again.

Outside, the city roared on, oblivious, while inside the days passed without meaning. Light filtered weakly through the drawn curtains, shifting from gray to black and back again. The clock on the wall, long since drained of its batteries, had stopped at some forgotten hour. Time no longer moved in the room.

She dreamed, sometimes, in short, feverish bursts. Dreams of hands pressing against her stomach, voices whispering too low to understand, the sensation of slipping underwater, deeper and deeper, until the weight of it became unbearable. Sometimes, she woke gasping, clutching at her ribs, drenched in sweat. Other times, she woke to nothing at all.

She had stopped looking at herself in the mirror. The one in the bathroom was cracked, a long, jagged fracture running down its center, distorting everything it reflected. She had caught a glimpse of herself once, days ago, and recoiled. The woman staring back had been a stranger with sunken eyes, lips colorless, hair hanging in limp, greasy strands. She had pressed her fingers to her face then, feeling the sharp angles of her cheekbones, the hollowness beneath them.

It had been the first time she had truly registered the decay.

The knock came again. Louder this time and more insistent.

Her hands gripped the sheets, stiff as parchment. A voice followed, muffled through the door.

"Carrie? Are you in there?"

The sound of her own name was foreign. It took her a moment to recognize it.

A pause. Then another knock, the handle rattling slightly. "I know you're in there. Open up."

Her throat was raw when she swallowed. How long had it been since she had spoken? Days? Longer? She licked her lips, her tongue catching on the cracks in her skin.

The knocking stopped. A long silence followed, stretching thin as thread. Then, a sigh. "I'll be back tomorrow. Please... just answer me next time."

More footsteps. The rustling of fabric, as though someone had left something at the door. Then quiet.

She stayed motionless for a long time after they had gone, staring at the ceiling. The shadows there moved like liquid, shifting, swirling. A slow, sinking feeling curled inside her ribs.

She had thought the worst of it was over. But perhaps she had only just begun to rot.

~

The afternoon light filtered through the trees in golden shafts, illuminating the clearing where Theo and Charlotte darted between thick trunks, their laughter ringing through the stillness of the woods. The scent of pine and warm earth filled the air, mingling with the distant salt of the sea. It was a perfect day. The kind that felt suspended in time, untouchable.

The woods stretched wide around them, ancient and full of secrets. Towering oaks and maples formed a cathedral of green, their branches weaving overhead, dappling the ground with light and shadow. The earth was soft underfoot, a bed of moss and fallen leaves, with tiny wildflowers peeking out between the roots. Birds flitted above them, their songs blending with the distant rustling of the wind through the treetops. The forest felt alive, carrying the scent of damp earth, crushed leaves, and the faint, almost sweet aroma of pine resin.

Isabel stood at the edge of the clearing, watching as Theo crouched behind a fallen log, his small hands pressing into the mossy bark. He had found the perfect hiding spot, but Charlotte, ever perceptive, was already creeping toward him, her dress billowing slightly in the breeze.

"You can't hide forever, Theo!" she called, giggling.

Isabel smiled, her heart swelling with something almost maternal as she watched them. In six months, they had become inseparable. The rigid, overly mannered children she had first met had softened into something warmer, something freer. They trusted her now, clung to her in a way that made her feel like more than just their nanny and more like something close to family.

Charlotte's triumphant shriek pierced the air as she pounced, wrapping her arms around her brother in victory. Theo let out a groan of mock defeat, collapsing onto the ground in dramatic fashion. Isabel approached, crouching beside them.

"Caught again?" she teased, ruffling Theo's dark curls.

"She's too fast," he said, breathless but grinning.

"I am not!" Charlotte declared. "You're just too slow."

They tumbled onto the grass, still laughing, and Isabel stretched out beside them, gazing up at the sky through the canopy of leaves. The sun was beginning to dip lower, its light turning a honeyed hue. The estate, though only a short walk away, felt distant here, as if they had entered another world entirely, one untouched by the coldness of Evelyn Lockwood or the indifference of Oliver.

Nearby, beyond the trees, the lake shimmered in the afternoon sun. It was vast, a mirror of rippling gold and sapphire, its surface dotted with floating leaves. The water stretched far beyond what they could see from here, bordered by reeds that swayed gently in the breeze. Every now and then, a dragonfly skimmed the water's edge, its iridescent wings flashing in the light.

Theo sat up suddenly, glancing toward the lake. "Let's go to the water," he said, his eyes bright with excitement.

Charlotte clapped her hands in delight. "Yes! Let's race!"

Before Isabel could answer, they were off, their small feet kicking up leaves and twigs as they darted between the trees. Laughing, Isabel chased after them, her dress catching on the underbrush as she ran. The sound of their footsteps echoed through the woods, their joy infectious.

When they reached the water's edge, Theo skidded to a stop, his breath coming fast. He dropped to his knees in the grass, pressing his hands to the cool earth. Charlotte followed, flopping down beside him, her fingers tracing patterns in the pebbles near the shore.

"It's so pretty," she murmured, her voice hushed as if speaking too loudly might disturb the magic of the moment.

Isabel sank down between them, smoothing Charlotte's tangled curls away from her face. "It is," she agreed. "Do you know how deep it is?"

Theo leaned forward, squinting at the water. "Papa says it's very deep in the middle. But I bet I could swim across it."

Charlotte gasped. "No, you couldn't!"

"I could," he insisted. "One day."

Isabel chuckled. "Maybe when you're a little older."

Theo huffed but didn't argue, instead dipping his fingers into the water and watching the ripples spread outward. Charlotte found a smooth, flat stone and stood, testing its weight in her palm. She pulled back her arm and sent it skipping across the surface one, two, three times before it sank beneath the water.

Theo gasped in delight. "Teach me how to do that!"

Charlotte grinned. "It's all in the wrist."

For the next hour, they took turns skipping stones, their laughter carrying across the water. Isabel watched them, soaking in the moment, memorizing the way the light caught in their hair, the way their smiles crinkled the corners of their eyes. It was perfect in a way life so rarely was.

As the sun dipped lower, casting long shadows across the lake, Isabel stood, brushing the dirt from her dress. "Come on, you two. It's time to head back."

The clearing was quieter now, the warmth of the afternoon shifting into the golden glow of early evening. Isabel let out a slow breath, glancing at the sky, where streaks of pink and lavender bled into one another. The air was cooler, tinged with the crisp scent of pine and damp earth. She knelt in the grass, gathering the toys the children had scattered in their excitement. Theo's small wooden plane, Charlotte's beloved stuffed rabbit with the frayed ear, a skipping rope curled like a serpent lay forgotten in the dirt.

She smiled to herself as she worked, relishing the simple joy of their laughter still echoing in her mind. That day had been a one of those rare, golden moments where time felt suspended, untroubled, untouched by anything outside their small world. But when she turned back, the children were gone.

Her smile faltered. Her pulse, steady and even just a moment before, skipped a beat

"Theo? Charlotte?"

Her voice was light, expectant. They were hiding. It wouldn't be the first time they had tried to sneak up on her, erupting into giggles when she "failed" to find them.

Silence.

She set the toys down and straightened, scanning the woods, searching for the telltale flash of Theo's blue sweater or Charlotte's pale dress among the dense green foliage. A prickle of unease crawled up the back of her neck.

"Theo!" she called again, louder this time. "Charlotte!"

Only the whisper of the wind through the trees answered her.

She took a few steps forward, peering between the trunks. The woods stretched out in all directions, dense and labyrinthine. The lake glistened in the distance, its surface rippling lazily in the breeze, but there was no sign of them near the water. Her heart thudded harder now, an insistent drumbeat beneath her ribs.

A game, she told herself. It's just a game. But the woods were too still.

Her voice cracked on the next call. "This isn't funny. Come out now."

Nothing.

A chill crept into her bones. She turned sharply, her breath quickening. She hadn't heard footsteps, hadn't heard their usual giggles. If this were a game, wouldn't they be peeking out by now, grinning, their hands clasped over their mouths to keep from laughing?

She dropped the toys without a second thought and took off toward the estate. The ground was uneven beneath her feet, roots jutting up from the earth like skeletal fingers, grasping at her ankles as she ran. Branches whipped against her arms, tugging at her dress. She stumbled once, catching herself against the trunk of a tree before pushing forward, breath ragged.

She needed to get to the house and away from the woods, away from the ominous hush that had settled over the trees. Each step carried her farther from the glistening lake, which shimmered like an unspoken warning behind her. It had seemed peaceful before, a place of joy and skipping stones, but now it loomed, vast and knowing, its waters swallowing all sound.

Isabel's legs burned as she ran, the estate growing larger ahead, its white facade glowing in the fading light. It felt impossibly far, the space between her and its towering walls stretching with each hurried step. Her breath came in shallow gasps. She needed help. Someone. Anyone. Evelyn. Oliver. The staff.

Her mind whirled with possibilities, each one worse than the last.

Theo and Charlotte were gone. And Isabel had no idea where to find them.

The lake shimmered ominously in the distance behind her.

10

PRESENT

The sky is a dull, muted gray. The kind that weighs on you, heavy and unrelenting. The air carries the sharp bite of approaching winter, and a cold wind slices through the yard, sending a shiver up my spine.

I wrap my arms around myself, shifting my weight from one foot to the other as I watch Noah play.

He's crouched in the grass near the sandbox, tracing patterns in the dirt with a stick. Every so often, he chatters to himself, completely immersed in whatever world he's creating.

I try to let myself relax, to soak in this moment. But I can't shake the feeling.

It's the same feeling I've had for days now. A prickling at the back of my neck, the faint unease curling in my stomach. Like I'm being watched.

I tell myself I'm just being paranoid. That it's nothing.

Still, my eyes flick toward the edges of the yard, scanning the fence line, the trees beyond it.

Nothing.

Just the quiet peace of the neighborhood. A dog barking

faintly down the street. The rustling of dry leaves skittering across the pavement.

My phone rings inside the house.

I turn toward the sound, hesitating only a second before stepping inside, leaving the sliding door cracked open just enough to hear Noah if he calls for me.

I grab the phone off the counter and glance at the screen.

Mom.

I exhale, pressing the phone to my ear. "Hey."

"Izzy, hi, sweetheart." Mom's voice is warm, familiar, but there's the usual thread of concern woven through it. "I just wanted to check in. You doing okay?"

I shift the phone to my other ear, peeking outside through the kitchen window. Noah is still there, his small figure bent in concentration.

"I'm fine," I say, forcing lightness into my tone. "Just... busy."

Mom tuts knowingly. "You always say that."

I smile faintly, grabbing a water glass from the drying rack. "Because it's always true."

"How's Noah?"

I glance back outside. "He's good. Playing in the yard. I told him we'd go to the park later, but now he's on his own schedule, apparently."

Mom chuckles. "Typical three-year-old. And Dan?"

"He's—" I pause, rubbing my forehead. "He's fine. Work's been stressful. And he's, um... he's worried about me."

There's a beat of silence.

Mom sighs. "What's going on, Izzy?"

I hesitate. I could tell her. I could voice the words sitting like lead in my chest. I could tell her that I'm scared, that something doesn't feel right, that I wake up in the middle of the night certain I heard footsteps where there shouldn't be any.

But I don't. Because if I say it out loud, it becomes real.

And I can't let it be real.

Instead, I shake my head, even though she can't see me. "It's nothing. Just… a lot on my mind."

Mom doesn't sound convinced, but she doesn't push. "You know I'm here, right? If you need to talk."

I swallow the lump in my throat. "I know."

I glance at the window again.

And freeze.

The yard is empty and my stomach drops.

I push the sliding door open and step out, gripping the phone tighter. "Mom, hold on."

The wind rushes past, scattering leaves across the grass. The air suddenly feels too sharp, too loud.

"Noah?" My voice wobbles, but I force it steady.

Silence.

I step further into the yard, my pulse kicking up.

He was just here.

"Noah," I call again, louder this time. "Sweetheart, come here."

Nothing.

A strange, hollow ringing fills my ears, drowning out everything else. My fingers dig into the phone, my breath coming too fast.

"Izzy?" Mom's voice is distant now, blurred at the edges. "What's wrong?"

I don't answer.

Because I already know. He's gone.

The phone is still pressed against my ear, Mom's voice distant and worried on the other end. But I can't focus on her words.

I can't focus on anything.

Because Noah is gone.

A sharp, electric fear surges through me, tightening my

chest, making my breath stutter. My grip on the phone tightens until my knuckles turn white.

"I—I have to call you back," I manage, my voice barely more than a whisper.

"Izzy? What's wrong?"

I don't answer. Instead I hang up.

The phone slips from my fingers, clattering onto the wooden porch as I step further into the yard, my legs unsteady beneath me.

He's hiding. He has to be hiding.

"Noah?" My voice is too loud, too high.

Silence.

My pulse slams in my ears as I start moving, my feet kicking through fallen leaves. My eyes scan the yard—desperate, searching for the tiny shape of my son crouching somewhere, giggling, waiting to jump out and yell *boo*!

But the yard is empty.

The wind stirs the trees, branches shifting like reaching fingers. The sandbox is still, his stick drawings undisturbed. The swing at the far end of the yard sways gently, empty, creaking softly in the wind.

"Noah, this isn't funny," I call again, my voice wobbling. "Come out, baby, please."

No sound. No movement.

A sickening déjà vu slams into me.

The Lockwood children.

I had called for them like this, too—voice breaking, feet moving faster, breath catching in my chest. Running through the grounds of the estate, searching every corner, every inch of land. Charlotte? Theo?

And they had never answered.

Just like Noah isn't answering now.

My stomach clenches violently, but I force myself to move.

I tear through the yard, pushing past the bushes at the edge of the fence, my hands trembling as I shove branches aside.

Nothing.

I run toward the trees lining the back of the property, peering between their trunks, my breath coming in sharp, shallow gasps.

Still nothing.

The world starts spinning, blurring at the edges, my vision tunneling.

He was just here. He was playing. He was laughing.

And now he's gone.

I spin on my heel and sprint back toward the house, my heart hammering so hard I feel like I might vomit.

He's inside. He *has to* be inside.

Maybe he ran in while I wasn't looking. Maybe he's playing a game, hiding under a table or behind the couch.

Please, God, let him be inside.

I stumble through the door, my foot catching on the threshold, nearly sending me sprawling.

"Noah?" My voice cracks.

I rush through the living room first. The couch is untouched, his favorite blanket still crumpled in the corner where he left it this morning. The TV hums quietly, its screen dark.

I lurch forward, yanking open the closet door. A row of coats greets me—motionless, undisturbed.

I slam it shut and move to the kitchen, my hands gripping the counter for balance. My lungs burn, my throat closing around each breath.

"Noah, baby, please," I plead, my voice strangled.

I drop to my knees and peer under the table, my fingers gripping the floor as if I can will him to be there. But the space is empty. Cold.

I stagger back up, nearly knocking over a chair as I move toward the hallway.

The bathroom.

I shove the door open so hard it bounces against the wall. The sink is dry, the towels neatly folded. The shower curtain is pulled back. The tub, empty.

I clutch the edge of the sink, my vision blurring.

He's not here.

I move to the stairs taking them two at a time, my pulse a deafening drumbeat in my ears.

His bedroom door is open.

I don't remember leaving it open.

I step inside, chest heaving, my hand grasping the doorframe to steady myself.

The bed is untouched, his stuffed animals propped against the pillows exactly as they were this morning. His toy cars are scattered across the rug, the ones he was playing with before we left for the store still lined up in a neat row.

But there's no sign of him.

I stumble back into the hall, my vision swimming.

The guest room. The bathroom. My own bedroom.

I throw open every door, searching, searching, searching.

He's nowhere.

I'm gasping now, my breaths shallow and panicked. My hands shake violently, my whole body trembling with the force of my fear.

This isn't real.

This can't be real.

I grip the hallway wall, pressing my forehead against the cool surface, trying to force myself to think.

The Lockwood children. They were gone before I could stop it. I will not let that happen again.

I push away from the wall, stumbling toward the stairs,

grabbing my phone from where I left it on the porch. My hands shake so badly I can barely press the buttons. I don't even realize I'm crying until my vision blurs completely, hot tears spilling down my cheeks as I press the phone to my ear.

Dan. The moment he picks up, I break.

"Dan," I sob, my voice strangled and desperate. "He's gone."

"Hey, Izzy, what did you say?"

I can't speak. My breath is coming too fast, too uneven, and for a split second, my voice refuses to work.

"Izzy?"

I force the words out, though they barely sound like my own. "Dan... he's gone."

There's a beat of silence.

A pause so long I think maybe the call has dropped, or maybe I didn't say it out loud at all. Maybe this is still some sick dream I haven't woken up from.

Then, Dan exhales sharply. "What?"

"Noah—" My throat closes around the words. "He's gone, Dan. He was just here, playing in the yard, and now he's—he's gone."

I hear the rustle of him shifting in his chair, the way his tone immediately changes—firmer, but not alarmed.

"Izzy, he's probably hiding," he says, like this is something we can fix, like this isn't the worst moment of my entire life unfolding in real time. "You know he likes to mess with you. Check behind the shed, or inside the house again."

I clench my jaw so hard it aches. "*I've checked everywhere.*"

"Izzy—"

"Don't Izzy me, Dan," I snap, my voice raw and shaking. "He is gone. I've looked under every bed, in every closet, behind every door. I ran through the whole goddamn yard, checked the bushes, the trees, the street. He's not here. *He's not here.*"

Dan exhales, like he's trying to keep me from spiraling, but I am spiraling. I am already there.

"Listen to me," he says carefully. "Kids do this. They wander. They hide, and they stay quiet because they think it's funny. He's done it before."

"Not like this," I choke out.

Another pause.

I can hear the clatter of his pen being dropped onto his desk. "Okay. Okay, take a breath. When did you last see him?"

I press a shaking hand to my forehead, gripping my hair. "I was watching him play in the yard. He was right there, Dan. I could see him. Then my phone rang. I was inside for seconds—" My voice cracks, and my grip tightens. "And when I came back, he was gone."

I hear Dan mutter something under his breath, his voice still measured. "Who called?"

I blink, thrown off. "What?"

"You said your phone rang. Who called?"

I shake my head, my mind scrambling. "My—my mom. Dan, it doesn't matter—"

"It does matter," he insists. "Because this doesn't mean someone took him. It means he might have walked off while you weren't looking. He could be anywhere, Izzy. You know how fast he moves. Maybe he..."

I feel something snap inside me, white-hot fury rising up to meet my fear. "Are you seriously standing there, telling me this is my fault?"

Dan exhales through his nose, frustration creeping into his voice. "That's not what I said."

"No, but that's what you meant. That I wasn't paying attention, that I let him wander off, that I lost him." My throat tightens painfully. "That I let this happen. Again."

Dan goes silent.

A horrible, gut-wrenching silence.

Then, carefully, "I didn't say that."

But he's thinking it. I know he is.

I squeeze my eyes shut, my entire body trembling, anger bubbling just beneath the surface.

"I'm not crazy, Dan," I whisper.

"I never said you were." But I can hear it, the way his voice is laced with something careful, something cautious, something wrong. Like he's already decided what's happening here. Like he doesn't believe me.

I tighten my grip on the phone. "Come home."

"Izzy—"

"Come home and see for yourself."

He hesitates. "I'm in the middle of a meeting—"

I nearly throw the phone. "Dan, I swear to God—"

"*Alright*." His voice sharpens. "Alright. I'm coming."

The line goes dead.

I stare at the phone in my shaking hand, my breath coming in ragged, uneven bursts.

I turn toward the yard again, my eyes locking onto the empty space where Noah should be.

A cold wind rushes past, slicing through my sweater, seeping into my bones.

Dan doesn't believe me. Not yet. But he will. Because Noah is gone. And someone took him.

11

SEVEN AND A HALF YEARS AGO

Isabel burst through the doors of the Lockwood estate, her breath coming in quick, shallow gasps, her heart hammering against her ribs. The cool air inside was a shock to her overheated skin, but she barely noticed. The moment she stepped into the grand marble foyer, the stillness struck her. The Lockwood house was always a quiet place, but now, in the wake of the children's sudden disappearance, the silence felt unnatural and stifling.

"Theo and Charlotte," she gasped, her gaze darting wildly between the staff members in the foyer. "I can't find them. They were just playing in the woods, and now they're gone."

Mr. Doyle, the butler, straightened sharply from his usual rigid stance by the staircase. He studied Isabel with narrowed eyes, as if waiting for her to catch her breath, to tell him this was all a misunderstanding.

But she didn't.

Mrs. Beckett, the cook, emerged from the hallway leading to the kitchens, her thick arms dusted with flour, a dishcloth clutched in one hand. "What are you saying, Miss Carter?" Her voice was sharper than usual, though not unkind, only laced with urgency.

"They were right there." Isabel could hardly breathe, her words tumbling out too fast, too desperate. "We were playing hide-and-seek. I turned away for a second to gather their things. When I looked back, they were gone."

The hush that followed was suffocating.

"We'll search the house," Mr. Doyle said suddenly, his voice clipped. "They may have come inside without you noticing."

Mrs. Beckett nodded quickly, turning to one of the wide-eyed maids lingering in the hallway. "Check the nursery and the playroom first. Then every other room. Go."

The house erupted into movement.

Isabel took the stairs two at a time, her stomach twisting into knots. Some deep, horrible part of her knew with certainty that Theo and Charlotte weren't in the house. But she had to look. She had to be sure.

She rushed into the nursery first, her eyes falling immediately on their beds, expecting to see Charlotte's small form curled beneath the blankets. But the bed was untouched, still neatly made from the morning. The dollhouse in the corner stood with its windows dark and empty. Charlotte's stuffed rabbit sat on the windowsill, staring blankly out into the fading light.

Isabel turned and moved quickly to the wardrobe, yanking the doors open with a breathless, silent prayer.

Nothing.

She crouched down, peering under the beds, her hands trembling as she lifted the bed skirts.

Empty.

A voice rang from the hall, one of the maids, breathless. "Not in the playroom."

Isabel forced herself to move, crossing the hall to the next room, throwing open doors with a desperation that mounted with each empty space.

The library was empty.

In the sunroom was only the ghost of late afternoon light spilling through the lace curtains.

They moved through the house in methodical, frantic steps, each unchecked room adding to the unbearable weight pressing on Isabel's chest.

The west wing.

The linen closets.

The attic, where dust motes floated in the shaft of light from a tiny window.

Nothing.

She was panting by the time she reached the ground floor, nearly colliding with Mrs. Beckett at the base of the stairs.

"Nowhere," Isabel managed, her voice barely above a whisper. "They aren't in the house."

Mrs. Beckett pressed her lips into a thin, grim line. "Then we search outside."

Isabel turned, already striding toward the back door when Mrs. Beckett's voice stopped her in her tracks.

"Wait."

Isabel turned slowly, dread coiling in her stomach.

"You have to call Mrs. Lockwood."

The words hit like a slap.

Evelyn.

She had hardly seen her employer since arriving at the estate. Evelyn was as much a presence as she was a ghost, gliding through the house with cool disinterest, rarely engaging with anyone unless she deemed it necessary.

And now Isabel had to tell her she had lost her children.

"She's at the club," Isabel murmured. "Playing tennis."

Mrs. Beckett's expression remained firm. "She needs to know."

Isabel swallowed hard, her fingers twitching at her sides. She didn't trust her voice enough to respond.

Instead, she turned, making her way toward the telephone mounted on the wall near the butler's pantry.

Her hands trembled as she reached for the receiver.

Outside, the sun sank lower, the sky bleeding into shades of bruised purple and deep amber. The trees cast long, dark shadows over the lawn. And somewhere beyond them, past the tree line, the lake lay still and silent, swallowing the last of the daylight.

Waiting.

Mrs. Beckett reached out, steady and firm, placing a heavy hand over Isabel's trembling fingers before she could lift the receiver.

"I'll call her."

Isabel looked up. The cook's face was set, her expression unreadable, but there was something almost—merciful—in her gaze.

"You go," Mrs. Beckett said, her voice low, urgent. "Help Mr. Doyle search the grounds. The longer we wait, the farther they could be."

For a brief moment, Isabel felt relief. But it was drowned out almost instantly by the gnawing panic twisting through her ribs like a vice.

A knot had formed in her stomach, thick and unrelenting.

She didn't waste time thanking Mrs. Beckett. There was no time. Instead, she spun on her heel and rushed out of the house, bursting through the back doors into the cooling evening air.

The moment she stepped outside, the reality of the situation gripped her fully.

The grounds stretched before her, endless in the twilight. The perfectly trimmed hedges, the vast emerald lawn sloping downward toward the woods, the gravel path winding around the house—everywhere she looked, shadows deepened, darkness pooling in corners where the last of the sunlight couldn't reach.

Her pulse pounded so hard she could hear it in her ears.

"Theo!" she called, her voice high, shrill with fear. "Charlotte!"

No answer.

The wind stirred through the trees, rustling the high grass and leaves. It was the only sound.

She forced herself to move, her legs stiff and aching from the tension seizing her body. She ran down the slope of the lawn, her heels sinking into the damp grass, breath coming in short, uneven gasps.

Ahead, Mr. Doyle stood like a dark silhouette against the trees, his posture rigid as he scanned the grounds.

"Anything?" she called as she approached, her voice hoarse from shouting.

Mr. Doyle turned, his face drawn tight. "Not yet," he admitted. "I sent the other staff around the gardens, checking every path, every hedge. I'm heading back to the woods now."

The woods. The last place she had seen them. The last place they had been.

Isabel swallowed down the rising bile in her throat.

"I'm coming with you," she said immediately.

Mr. Doyle didn't argue. He simply nodded once, then turned and strode toward the looming trees, Isabel close behind.

As they neared the entrance to the woods, Isabel felt the air shift, cooler, damp, thick with the scent of moss and earth. The trees pressed in around them, their trunks gnarled and black in the dimming light.

Isabel's throat was raw, but she called out again, desperation cracking through every syllable.

"Theo! Charlotte!"

She listened. Nothing.

The hush of the woods was unnatural, eerie in a way that made her skin prickle. Panic crawled up her spine. She cupped her hands around her mouth, her voice breaking as she shouted once more.

"Theo! Charlotte!"

No laughter. No giggles. No hurried footsteps rushing toward her. Just silence. And beyond it, through the trees, the dark shimmer of the lake.

At first, it was just a sound. Distant, almost indistinguishable from the rustling wind. A voice, sharp and panicked, rising above the hush of the evening. Then another, more frantic. A cry.

Then a splash.

Isabel froze mid-step. The breath in her lungs turned to ice.

Her body knew before her mind did.

The lake.

She couldn't see it yet, hidden behind the thick black silhouettes of the trees but it was there, waiting. An unspoken force drawing her forward, an invisible hand curled around her throat.

Another splash. A shriek.

Her feet felt impossibly heavy, as if filled with stone. She forced herself forward, each step dragging, the damp earth sucking at her shoes, as though the ground itself wanted to hold her back. The world had gone dark at the edges, the trees stretching taller, their shadows shifting in unnatural ways.

Then, the trees broke. And she saw.

The lake lay before her, its surface rippling from recent movement, black as oil under the deepening twilight. The air smelled different here. She could almost taste the damp reeds, wet earth, something metallic and murky. The wind had picked up, and the water lapped at the edges, small waves licking the shore.

Figures moved frantically near the edge.

A woman stood in the lake, waist-deep, her dress sodden and heavy against her frame, her shoulders shaking with silent sobs. Her hands clutched something small, something pale, cradling it against her chest with a grip so tight her knuckles gleamed white even in the dim light.

Isabel couldn't breathe. She barely noticed her feet moving, the uneven ground beneath her as she stumbled forward, her vision narrowing to the scene before her.

On the bank, just beyond the water's edge, Mr. Doyle knelt in the dirt, his posture rigid, his arms wrapped around another small, unmoving body.

Theo.

His dark curls clung to his forehead, his skin leeched of warmth, his lips slightly parted as if caught mid-breath.

But he was not breathing.

A sound tore from Isabel's throat. Something inhuman, something desperate. Her legs buckled.

Mr. Doyle did not look up. His hands trembled slightly where they rested against the boy's still frame, but his expression remained eerily blank, as if his mind had already left this moment, as if he were just a body holding another body.

In the lake, the maid's sobs grew louder, shaking, raw. She rocked on her feet, still clutching Charlotte against her chest, her fingers digging into the girl's small, limp body.

Charlotte's pale dress clung to her, soaked through, her bare arms dangling lifelessly, one tiny hand curled as if she had been grasping for something before the end.

A scream tore through Isabel.

She moved without thinking, her hands reaching forward, as if touching them—holding them—could undo what had already happened.

The water. They had been in the water.

She turned, her gaze snapping to the surface of the lake. The ripples had begun to settle, smoothing out as if nothing had ever disturbed them at all. As if the lake had swallowed them whole and spat them back out, emptied of life.

Behind her, the maid was trembling, whispering something under her breath. A prayer, or perhaps a plea.

Isabel swallowed down bile again. The woods loomed behind them, dark and cavernous.

And there, just beyond the tree line, barely visible in the encroaching night, stood a figure.

Dripping wet. Still. Watching.

It didn't move. Didn't react. Just watched, unseen.

The wind shifted, and the surface of the lake shivered, a ripple spreading outward, brushing the shore like a whisper of something unspeakable.

In that moment, something in Isabel broke.

She turned back to the lifeless children before her and the dusk swallowed another scream.

12

7 AND A HALF YEARS AGO

Two days had passed.

The Lockwood estate stood silent.

Not the kind of silence that brings peace, comfort, or stillness. This was a silence so thick it pressed against the walls, sank into the carpets, and wrapped around the throats of those still inside like an unseen hand. A silence that smothered.

Outside, beyond the grand iron gates, the world had erupted in noise.

The press had descended like vultures, cameras flashing in violent bursts against the early morning fog. The pavement outside the estate was littered with cables, microphones, and discarded coffee cups. Reporters shouted questions, their voices rising and falling in desperate waves, each one fighting to be the loudest, the most intrusive.

"Miss Carter! Isabel Carter—why haven't you made a statement?"

"Where were you in those last moments?"

"Do you believe you could have saved them?"

The last one landed like a slap.

Isabel sat in the dim drawing room, the heavy drapes pulled

just enough to glimpse them and their eager, hunched forms waiting, lenses sharp and ready, mouths twisted with a strange, gleeful hunger.

They wanted a villain. And they had found one.

She turned away from the window, her stomach twisting. The room felt suffocating, too large and too empty all at once. The polished mahogany furniture gleamed, untouched. The fireplace was cold, the embers long since faded.

She hadn't slept. Not really.

When she closed her eyes, she saw the lake. Black water lapping at the shore, ripples distorting the stillness, breaking it apart. Charlotte's dress, soaked and clinging. Theo's curls plastered to his cold forehead.

She pressed her palms to her eyes, forcing the images away.

Somewhere in the house, someone moved. She heard light footsteps against the marble floors. The staff had barely spoken in the last forty-eight hours. They moved as though underwater, slow and mechanical, their faces blank, hands carrying trays of untouched tea, untouched meals.

Mrs. Beckett had been in the kitchen since morning, though no one had eaten. The silver teapots, fine china, and linen napkins, all of it sat pristine and useless on the long dining table.

No one sat there. No one dared.

She thought of Evelyn, locked away in her bedroom upstairs, doors firmly closed. She hadn't come down since the police had left. Hadn't spoken. The only sign of life was the faint murmur of voices beyond the door, the occasional whisper of movement—her lady's maid tending to her, trying to restore some semblance of order to a world undone.

Oliver had returned late the night before. He'd gone straight to his study, slamming the door behind him. The staff had all heard the sound of glass breaking at some point during the night, but no one had gone in. No one had dared.

Isabel swallowed hard, throat dry, eyes burning.

She could still hear the voices outside.

"She was alone with them. That's what they're saying."

"She was the last one to see them alive."

"She should have been watching them."

She squeezed her eyes shut.

The words had followed her since the moment she returned to the house from the lake, since the police had questioned her, since the reporters had begun assembling outside like a pack of wolves circling fresh blood.

She had told the truth. She had turned for only a moment. She had called for them. She had searched. She had run.

But it hadn't mattered.

She let out a slow, shaking breath and opened her eyes. Across the room, Mr. Doyle stood by the grand mantelpiece, his back straight, hands clasped tightly in front of him. His usual composure had cracked in the first few hours after they returned from the lake, but now, he was a statue again.

Only his eyes betrayed him.

They were red-rimmed, heavy with something that went beyond grief.

"Mr. Doyle," Isabel rasped, surprised by how hoarse her voice was.

He turned to look at her, but it took him a moment before he spoke. When he did, his voice was quieter than she had ever heard it.

"They won't leave," he murmured, his gaze flicking toward the window, where the reporters still lingered. "Not until they get what they came for."

She understood what he meant.

They wanted someone to blame. And she was the easiest target.

Isabel pushed herself to her feet. The exhaustion clung to her like wet fabric, making her limbs feel heavier than they should. She moved toward the window again, the gap in the curtains just wide enough for her to see the crowd, which had grown larger, the flashing cameras an endless, nauseating flicker.

The outside world would never let this go. It had only just begun.

Upstairs, the television flickered in the dimly lit bedroom, casting a pale, shifting glow over the silk wallpaper and the heavy drapes drawn tight against the outside world. The screen was filled with faces—reporters standing in the rain-dampened gravel outside the Lockwood estate, their microphones poised, their voices practiced and solemn.

Evelyn Lockwood sat perfectly still on the edge of her chaise lounge, her robe cinched tightly at the waist, the untouched remnants of her morning tea cooling on the side table beside her.

She had barely moved in two days.

The world had not stopped turning, though hers had. The world had not fallen into silence, though her house had. The world had not lost everything, though she had.

On the screen, the news anchor's voice was smooth and clear, almost clinical.

"The deaths of Theo and Charlotte Lockwood have sparked widespread speculation over the role of their nanny, Isabel Carter, who was reportedly the last person to see them alive. Carter, who has worked for the Lockwood family for six months, was alone with the children at the time of their disappearance. The question remains, was this a tragic accident? Or was there negligence at play?"

Evelyn's hand tightened on the fabric of her robe.

Isabel.

The camera cut to an image of the estate gates, swarming with the press. Then to another of an older photograph of Isabel, taken from what must have been an employee record, her face frozen in time with an easy, open smile.

"Sources close to the family report that Mrs. Lockwood is devastated by the loss of her children, though she has yet to make a public statement. Mr. Lockwood, seen leaving his office late last night, declined to comment."

Evelyn let out a slow, trembling breath.

She had barely seen Oliver. He had locked himself in his study, drinking, avoiding. That was what he did. He had been a ghost in their marriage, and now he was a ghost in their grief.

But Isabel was still here.

Still inside this house.

The screen flashed again, this time showing a video taken earlier that day. Reporters shoving microphones at the estate's iron gates, demanding answers, speculation mounting in real time. A woman's voice rang out over the footage.

"She was supposed to be watching them."

Something inside Evelyn snapped.

She rose to her feet, her breath coming too quickly, her vision edged with something dark and furious. The floor felt unsteady beneath her, but she moved anyway, yanking open the door to her bedroom and stepping into the silent, cold corridor.

She hadn't left this room since that night. She had hidden away, locked in a cage of her own making, wrapped in silk, grief, and nothingness. But now she was moving.

And she was going to find her.

The hallway stretched before her, long and empty, the house impossibly still. She could hear the faint murmur of voices from below, the hushed, exhausted movements of the staff. She followed the sound, her breath ragged, her fingers gripping the railing as she descended the grand staircase.

She found Isabel in the drawing room.

The girl stood near the window, the curtain slightly drawn, her shoulders tense. She must have heard Evelyn approaching, but she didn't turn.

Evelyn stopped in the doorway, her pulse pounding against her ribs.

"Get out."

The words cut through the silence like a knife.

Isabel turned slowly, her face pale, her eyes red-rimmed, hollow. She opened her mouth, but no sound came out.

Evelyn took a step closer, her breath shuddering. "Get out of my house."

Isabel flinched, her fingers tightening around the curtain.

Evelyn didn't stop. She didn't care.

"You were supposed to take care of them," she whispered, her voice breaking. "You were supposed to protect them."

Isabel shook her head, her lips trembling. "I—"

"They are dead." Evelyn's voice rose, raw and shaking, her composure fracturing like glass. "My children are dead. And you," her breath hitched. "You let it happen."

Isabel took a small, desperate step forward, hands raised slightly, as if she could fix this, as if she could rewind time.

"I didn't—"

"GO."

Evelyn screamed it this time, the force of it ripping from her throat, echoing through the vast, empty house.

Isabel stood frozen, her face twisted in something between horror and grief.

Evelyn felt something hot slide down her cheek. She didn't reach up to wipe it away.

She hadn't cried. Not properly. Not since the night at the

lake. Not when the police came. Not when the press arrived. Not until now.

Because now, she could feel it. She could feel the absence of them. Their laughter. Their voices. Their warmth.

And the only person left to blame was standing in front of her.

"Get out," she whispered one last time.

And this time, Isabel moved.

Isabel didn't remember packing her belongings, but she was outside now, by the back entrance, where the press couldn't see her, the sharp evening air biting at her skin, her breath coming in short, panicked bursts. The house loomed behind her, dark and silent, a fortress of grief and blame that had expelled her like a disease.

Mr. Doyle waited by the car. He didn't speak.

He simply opened the passenger door of the sleek black sedan, his expression impassive, his usual composure intact. But there was something different in his posture, something heavy, something resigned.

Isabel hesitated, glancing once over her shoulder, back toward the grand house where she had lived for six months, back toward the rooms where she had read bedtime stories, tied shoelaces, wiped away tears, and kissed scraped knees.

Where Theo and Charlotte no longer were.

She swallowed the lump in her throat and got into the car. The door shut behind her with a soft, final click.

Mr. Doyle rounded the front of the vehicle and slid into the driver's seat. Without a word, he started the ignition. The engine purred to life, smooth and expensive, and the gravel beneath the tires crunched as they rolled down the long driveway, away from the house, away from everything.

Isabel pressed her forehead to the cool glass of the window.

Beyond the iron gates, beyond the manicured lawns, she

could see the reporters. A sea of cameras and flashing lights, bodies shifting, eager, waiting.

She was leaving through the back entrance. They would never see her go.

And in her place, they would be given something better.

A spectacle. A sacrifice. A villain.

Evelyn stood before the mirror, her hands steady as she ran a silver comb through her hair.

The movements were practiced, controlled, precise.

There were no tremors in her fingers, no redness around her eyes. She had wiped away the evidence, reapplied her makeup with the same careful deliberation she always used. Powder to smooth the skin. Lipstick in a shade that neither screamed nor whispered. A thin line of kohl to frame her blue eyes—cool, unfeeling, unreadable.

Behind her, the door remained ajar, and somewhere beyond it, the house continued to hold its breath.

Oliver had not emerged from his study.

She had not expected him to.

This was hers to handle.

She set the comb down gently on the vanity table, smoothing the front of her dress before rising to her feet. She turned toward the window, where the glow of press cameras flickered against the dark.

They were waiting.

And she would give them what they wanted.

The moment Evelyn stepped out onto the front steps, the air shifted.

The chaos of voices, the clamor of bodies pushing against the barriers, the flashing of cameras all stilled, if only for a moment, as they took her in.

She did not look broken.

She did not look like a grieving mother, hollowed out by loss, shattered by pain. She looked composed. Unshaken. Cold.

It was what they had come for.

The microphones extended, reporters leaning in, desperate, their voices rising like a tide.

"Mrs. Lockwood, do you believe your children were victims of foul play?"

"Is it true that the nanny has been dismissed?"

"Do you hold her responsible?"

Evelyn let them speak. Let them boil over with questions, let the words fill the space with accusation, heavy with expectation.

Then, she raised a single hand, palm outward. The noise cut. Silence.

And then, in a voice as smooth and detached as glass, she spoke.

"My husband and I are devastated by the loss of our children." She paused, letting the words settle, her expression placid, her breath measured. "We are cooperating fully with the authorities to understand what happened that day."

A murmur rippled through the crowd. A camera clicked.

Evelyn lifted her chin slightly, her next words falling like stones.

"As of today, our children's former nanny has been dismissed from our employment. Given the circumstances, we believe it is necessary to bring our concerns regarding her negligence to the police."

The reaction was immediate. Reporters scrambled, voices overlapping, pens scratching against notepads, cameras zooming in.

Evelyn did not react. She simply turned her gaze toward the flashing lights, her eyes catching the glow, reflecting nothing.

She had played her part. And she would let the world do the rest.

Across town, in a dimly lit apartment thick with the scent of stale air and forgotten time, Carrie sat curled on the sagging couch, the television casting flickering shadows across the cluttered room. The blue glow bathed her face, accentuating the sharp angles of her cheekbones and the dark smudges beneath her eyes.

She hadn't moved much in the past two days.

Her body ached from the stillness, herlimbs stiff, skin clammy. She barely registered the cold cup of tea sitting untouched on the coffee table or the crust of a sandwich she had made but never eaten.

She had been waiting for this moment.

The news had been relentless images of the grand Lockwood estate, iron gates swarmed by reporters, and a grainy photograph of Isabel Carter smiling, her hair tucked behind her ears, frozen in time before it all fell apart. The anchors speculated in smooth, deliberate tones, their voices coiling through the room like smoke.

"How could this happen?"

"The Lockwoods have dismissed their nanny in the wake of the tragedy."

"Police are investigating allegations of negligence."

Carrie exhaled slowly, her fingers tightening around the blanket draped over her lap.

Then the screen shifted.

Evelyn Lockwood. Stepping onto the front steps of her estate composed, elegant, cold.

Carrie leaned forward, breath catching in her throat.

She listened as Evelyn spoke, each syllable clipped and precise, the weight of her words sharp enough to carve stone.

"As of today, our children's former nanny has been dismissed from

our employment. Given the circumstances, we believe it is necessary to bring forward our concerns regarding her negligence to the police."

Carrie stared. Then, slowly, she nodded.

"Yes," she murmured, her lips barely moving.

Her fingers traced absent patterns against the fabric of the couch, eyes still fixed on the screen, unblinking.

"Yes, Isabel is to blame," she said again, firmer this time. "She wasn't watching the children."

Her voice was calm. Matter-of-fact.

She blinked once, slowly, then reached for the remote and turned up the volume. She wanted to hear it again.

13

PRESENT

The police arrive within twenty minutes.

The sirens are silent, but the presence of two patrol cars and an unmarked vehicle outside the house feels louder than if they had blared through the entire neighborhood. Red and blue lights flicker against the early evening sky, bouncing off the windows, turning my kitchen into something eerie and foreign.

I stand by the counter, arms wrapped tightly around myself, my stomach churning.

Dan is back now. He rushed through the door, his tie loosened, his shirt wrinkled, his eyes filled with something I can't quite place. Not fear. Not yet.

Doubt.

It's always doubt with him.

Detective Birch is the last to step inside. He's in his late forties, built like a man who used to play football and still works out just enough to pretend his body isn't betraying him. His sharp brown eyes sweep the house, already cataloging everything, piecing together a story before I even open my mouth.

His gaze lands on me. "Mrs. Warren."

I nod stiffly, my throat too tight to speak.

Dan steps forward, shaking the detective's hand. "Detective Birch. Thanks for coming so quickly."

Birch nods once, then glances at the officers standing near the door. "Can we sit down?"

Dan gestures toward the dining table. I move automatically, pulling out a chair, my hands gripping the edge like it's the only thing keeping me upright.

"Alright," Birch says, taking a seat across from me and flipping open a notepad. "Let's start from the beginning. When did you last see your son?"

My breath is shallow. "An hour ago. Maybe less. He was playing in the yard."

Birch nods, making a note. "And then?"

I swallow. "Then my phone rang. I stepped inside—just for a second. When I came back, he was gone."

Birch's eyes flick to Dan, who stands stiffly by the table. "How long was she inside?"

Dan hesitates. "She said a few seconds."

Birch nods, his face unreadable.

I grip the table harder. "Someone took him."

Birch studies me carefully. "Did you see anyone?"

"No." My voice is hoarse. "But I know someone was watching. There were—" I stop abruptly, my stomach twisting.

"Mrs. Warren?"

I hesitate, my pulse hammering. I don't want to say it. But I have to.

"There were notes."

Birch's pen stills. "Notes?"

I nod quickly, the words rushing out. "Someone's been leaving them. First, they asked if I knew where Noah was. Then, the next one said—" My throat closes around the words.

Birch leans in slightly. "What did it say?"

I force myself to speak. "It said, He is mine."

A flicker of something crosses Birch's face, but he schools it quickly. "Do you still have these notes?"

I hesitate. The air in the room feels heavier, pressing in on me. I shake my head.

Birch frowns. "You don't have them?"

I swallow hard. "I, I threw them away."

The silence that follows is deafening.

Birch blinks. "You threw them away?"

I nod. "I wasn't thinking. I was scared."

Dan exhales sharply beside me. "Jesus, Izzy."

I snap my head toward him, my breath catching. His face is tight, his jaw clenched. But it's his eyes that get me.

Suspicion. I feel it like a slap.

"You didn't mention that," he says, his voice low, almost careful. "When I got home, you didn't tell me you threw them away."

I shake my head frantically. "I didn't think it mattered."

"Didn't matter?" Dan lets out a hollow laugh, running a hand through his hair. "Jesus Christ, Izzy. If someone was leaving threatening messages about our son, why the hell would you destroy the only evidence?"

"I wasn't thinking," I whisper, but even I know how thin it sounds.

Birch watches me with sharp, assessing eyes. "So, to be clear, you received anonymous threats, and instead of keeping them, you threw them away?"

"Yes," I croak.

Birch exchanges a glance with the officer beside him. I don't miss the way his expression shifts, the way something changes.

I can feel myself unraveling. Panic presses against my ribs, clawing to get out.

"Izzy," Dan says, his voice tense, frustrated. "You need to start making sense."

I can't breathe. I squeeze my eyes shut. "It's happening again," I whisper.

Dan stiffens. "What?"

I open my eyes, my vision blurring. "It's happening again. Just like before. Just like *Theo and Charlotte.*"

Silence. Thick. Heavy.

Detective Birch frowns. "Who?"

Dan exhales harshly, rubbing his temples. "Christ." He looks up at Birch, his expression pained. "There was an incident. Years ago."

Birch sits back slightly. "What kind of incident?"

Dan hesitates. I see it on his face. He doesn't want to say it. Birch's pen pauses mid-air.

The house feels smaller now.

The walls seem closer, the air heavier, the weight of too many eyes pressing down on me. I feel them all watching, Detective Birch, the officers, Dan.

And I hear my own voice, muttering under my breath, repeating their names like an incantation.

"Theo and Charlotte," I whisper, my fingers digging into my palms.

Detective Birch narrows his eyes slightly. "Who?"

I barely hear him.

Because I'm there again. At the Lockwood estate. Running through the corridors, tearing through the trees, my breath ragged, my heart pounding in my ears. Calling their names, *pleading* for them to come back, even when I already knew.

"Izzy," Dan says, his voice sharper now. "Stop."

I meet his gaze.

He looks exhausted, like he's carrying something too heavy, something he doesn't want to touch.

The detective leans forward slightly. "Dan," he says, his voice calm, measured. "What is she talking about?"

Dan exhales slowly, rubbing his temples before lifting his gaze back to Birch.

"There was an incident with a family," he starts, his voice lower now, careful. "Years ago. Two kids... they drowned."

Detective Birch tilts his head. "What family?"

Dan hesitates, then exhales. "The Lockwoods."

Birch's expression changes. His posture shifts, his shoulders stiffening slightly, eyes flicking to me with something unreadable.

Something colder.

I already know what's coming before he even says it.

"Oh." He nods slowly. "The Lockwood case."

A heavy silence settles over the room.

Dan clears his throat, his voice firm, rehearsed. "It was a tragic accident."

Birch doesn't say anything. The other officers exchange glances.

I stare at the detective, at the way his eyes flick over me differently now—assessing, calculating. Like I've shifted into something else entirely. Like I was one thing when he walked in, a mother with a missing child. Now I'm a question mark.

I see it happening in real time. His tone changes. His expression cools.

"You were involved?" Birch asks, and there's something in his voice, something distant.

I don't answer. Because I already know how this works.

I know what people see when they look at me and hear the name Lockwood.I know how fast trust dissolves.

Dan clears his throat. "She was their nanny."

Birch nods, as if that answers something for him. As if it confirms something.

I grip the table harder, my breath coming too fast.

"Two children," I say quietly, my voice hollow. "Gone." I swallow thickly. "And now it's happening again."

Birch studies me carefully. "Is it?"

His tone is mild. But I hear it. I hear it.

Not *We will find your son*. Not *This is just a coincidence*. Just a quiet, pointed question. As if Noah vanishing and my past colliding in the worst possible way was expected. As if they've already made up their minds about me. And I know, with bone-deep certainty that they don't think they're here to help me. They think they're here to watch me.

The air in the room shifts.

It's subtle. A glance, a hesitation, a softening of posture but I feel it like a blade against my skin.

They're looking at me differently now. Not as a mother with a missing child. As something else. As something suspect.

I won't let this happen again. I won't let them think, *for even a second*, that this is my fault.

I push back my chair, the legs scraping loudly against the wooden floor.

"No," I say, my voice stronger now, cutting through the thick silence.

Birch tilts his head slightly, like I've surprised him. "No?"

"No," I repeat. My hands slam onto the table. I force myself to breathe, to stay composed, but the panic is clawing at my ribs, desperate to take over.

I can't let it. Not now.

"My son is missing," I say, my voice trembling with fury. "And you're sitting here looking at me like I had something to do with it."

Birch doesn't react. Doesn't even blink.

"Mrs. Warren, no one is saying that."

I let out a humorless laugh. "Aren't you?" I gesture wildly.

"You walked in here, took notes, asked questions, and for a moment I thought, *finally*. Finally, someone is going to help me."

My voice cracks, but I don't stop.

"And then I mentioned the Lockwoods, and suddenly, everything changed."

Dan shifts beside me, uncomfortable. "Izzy—"

I turn on him. "Don't," I snap. "Don't tell me to calm down. Don't act like I don't see what's happening here."

I turn back to Birch, my breath shaking. "I know how this works. I know how people like you think."

Birch leans back slightly, watching me carefully, like he's measuring something unseen. "And how do we think?"

"You think it's easier," I spit. "You think it's easier to believe I'm lying, or that I did something, because that means this isn't random. That means there's a reason for this. But there isn't."

I shake my head violently. "You want to talk about the Lockwoods? Fine. Let's talk about them. Let's talk about how I was torn apart in the press, how everyone looked at me like I was a monster, how *I searched for those kids too*. How I loved them."

My throat is raw, but I push forward. "And now it's my son."

I press a shaking hand to my chest. "You don't get to turn this into something else. You don't get to waste time second-guessing me while he's out there."

A beat of silence. The room is thick with unspoken words.

Birch studies me for a long moment. Dan shifts beside me, rubbing a hand over his jaw, his shoulders tense.

Then, finally, Birch speaks. "Mrs. Warren, I understand this is incredibly distressing for you, but we have to consider every angle—"

"No." I shake my head interupting. "You have to find my son."

Birch exhales through his nose, closing his notepad. "We

have officers searching the neighborhood as we speak. We're checking surveillance footage, doorbell cameras—"

"It's not enough." My voice wobbles, and I shove my hands through my hair, gripping at my scalp. "Whoever left those notes, whoever was watching me—they took him."

Birch exchanges a glance with the officer beside him. "We have no evidence of that yet."

I clench my jaw. "Because I threw away the notes?"

Birch doesn't answer.

And suddenly, I realize something.

They're not moving fast enough. They don't believe me. They're treating this like a missing person case, not a kidnapping.

I shake my head, stepping back. "You don't believe me."

Dan's voice is cautious. "Izzy, that's not—"

I let out a choked sound, somewhere between a laugh and a sob. "You don't believe me," I whisper. "None of you do."

The panic rises again. I feel it. The overwhelming, all-consuming terror that something is happening right now, that every second wasted is another second my son is getting further away.

I turn toward the door. "I'll find him myself."

Dan moves quickly, stepping in front of me. "Whoa, whoa Izzy." He grips my arms, trying to steady me. "You need to breathe."

"No," I shove him away. "I need to find him. Because if you won't, if the police won't..."

I push past him, making it to the door before Birch speaks again.

"We are looking for him, Mrs. Warren."

I stop. My breath is ragged. My hands are shaking. I turn slowly.

Birch stands there, arms crossed, his expression unreadable.

"There are patrols out now. If someone took your son, we will find him."

Something about the way he says it makes my skin crawl. Because it's not just a promise. It's a warning. A warning that if they don't find someone else responsible— they will look at me.

I stare at him, my pulse hammering.

Dan exhales, rubbing his temples. "Izzy, please. Just let them do their jobs."

I shake my head, something desperate clawing at my throat.

"They don't think I need help," I whisper.

Dan frowns. "What?"

"They think I need *watching*."

No one responds. But no one denies it, either. And that silence tells me everything I need to know.

Detective Birch watches me carefully, his expression unreadable. I can feel the weight of his scrutiny, the way he's assessing everything. My words, my body language, the way my fingers tremble against the table.

"Mrs. Warren," he says finally, his voice even, professional. "Is there anywhere your son might have gone on his own? A friend's house? A favorite place? A playground?"

I shake my head automatically. "He wouldn't have left the yard."

"But if he did," Birch presses, his gaze sharpening. "Where would he go?"

I open my mouth, then hesitate. The playground. The one he always begs me to take him to. The one I promised we'd go to yesterday before the note, before everything went wrong. Before I kept him inside.

Oh, God. What if he got it in his head to go on his own?

What if I did this?

I yank my phone out of my pocket, my fingers fumbling as I scroll through my contacts. I barely hear Birch asking Dan something else, barely feel the way my breath comes too fast, my heartbeat pounding as I press call on Claire's name.

The line rings twice before she picks up.

"Izzy?" Her voice is bright at first, then quickly shifts, sensing something off. "What's wrong?"

My throat is dry. "Noah, he's missing. I don't know where he is. I," My voice cracks, and I press my palm hard against the counter, grounding myself. "I need to know if you've seen him."

"What?" There's rustling on the other end, like she's moving, grabbing something. "Noah's missing? How?"

"I don't know." My voice is hoarse, desperate. "One second he was in the yard, the next he was just gone." I squeeze my eyes shut. "The police are here. They're asking where he might have gone, and I, I don't know, Claire. I don't know."

There's silence for half a beat.

Then Claire says, "I'm going to the playground."

My eyes snap open.

"The one you always take him to?" she continues. "If he went anywhere on his own, it's there. I'll check and call you the second I see anything."

I nod frantically, even though she can't see me. "I'll meet you there."

"Izzy—"

But I don't hear the rest. I end the call, my body already moving before I can think, before I can breathe.

"Where are you going?" Dan demands as I grab my car keys from the counter.

I barely look at him. "To the playground."

"Izzy,"

I push past him, my heartbeat loud in my ears. "Stay here in case he comes back."

I don't wait for an answer. I bolt out the door, shoving my keys into the ignition with shaking hands. I have to get there. I have to find him. Because if I don't...

I can't even let myself finish the thought.

14

7 YEARS AGO

The sky was the color of wet ash. A dull, endless gray, heavy and suffocating. The city had been gripped by an unrelenting cold for weeks now, the streets lined with frozen puddles that cracked under hurried footsteps, the scent of old snow mixing with car exhaust and something metallic in the air.

Inside a cramped, dimly lit café on the corner of a quiet street, Carrie sat alone.

She had been there for hours, her chair tucked against the same small table near the window, her fingers curled around a chipped ceramic mug that had long since gone cold. The air inside smelled of burnt coffee and a faint trace of cinnamon from pastries sitting stale in the glass case near the register.

A small radio was mounted on the wall above the counter, playing a low, crackling news broadcast between bursts of static.

Carrie barely noticed the passing of time anymore.

She had watched the investigation unfold with a silent, obsessive fixation, following every update, reading every article, cutting and collecting headlines until they littered her apartment like discarded confetti. She had memorized the phrases journalists loved to use, absorbed the speculation, the endless back-and-forth between tragedy and blame.

For months, she had lived inside the Lockwood case.

The coroner's report had been released weeks ago. Official cause of death: drowning. The details were clinical, devoid of emotion. Hypothermia would have set in almost instantly. Theo and Charlotte Lockwood would have felt the freezing grip of the water, their small bodies dragged under, lungs filling with darkness before their hearts simply stopped.

Carrie had read it over and over. But still, it hadn't been enough. Nothing would be enough until Isabel Carter had paid for it.

She had been the last person to see them alive. She had been the one responsible for their safety. And yet.

Carrie's fingers tensed around the mug, her knuckles aching from the pressure.

The radio crackled again, the static shifting, and then a smooth voice, deliberate and impersonal, cut through the stale café air.

"In breaking news, sources confirm that former nanny Isabel Carter has been cleared of all charges in the deaths of Theo and Charlotte Lockwood. Authorities have concluded there is insufficient evidence of negligence, and the case will not move forward to prosecution. Carter, who has been in hiding since the tragedy, has yet to make a statement."

A long pause followed. Carrie blinked.

The words hung in the air dense and inescapable.

Cleared. Isabel Carter had been cleared.

Carrie sat motionless, her breath thin and sharp, her vision suddenly blurring at the edges.

This was wrong.

The world around her continued moving, unaffected by the unbearable pressure building in her chest. The waitress wiped down the counter. A man in a suit muttered something to his colleague over his newspaper. A couple sat in the corner, sharing a pastry, their laughter light and careless.

It felt obscene.

Carrie swallowed, but her throat was raw, burning as though something inside her was trying to claw its way out.

Her heart pounded in a frantic, irregular beat. The radio droned on.

"Carter's legal team has not responded to requests for comment, though public opinion remains divided on the role of negligence in this case. The Lockwoods, who dismissed Carter in the immediate aftermath of their children's deaths, released a brief statement today confirming that they will not be pursuing further legal action at this time."

That was it. That was all. It was over.

A strangled noise escaped her throat before she even realized it. Her hands were shaking. Her limbs felt weightless, unmoored, as though her body no longer belonged to her.

The café was suddenly too loud, too bright. Every sound was distorted, warped, pressing against her skull like a vise. The clink of a spoon against ceramic sent a jolt through her spine. The low rumble of the espresso machine buzzed in her ears like static.

She couldn't be there. She had to get out.

The chair scraped violently against the floor as she shoved back from the table, the force of it making the ceramic mug tip, coffee spilling in a slow, ugly stain across the table.

She barely noticed.

She was moving before she had even made the decision to stand, her legs carrying her toward the door, her breath coming in short, erratic gasps.

"Miss?" The waitress's voice barely registered, concern flickering across her face.

Carrie ignored her, shoved the door open, and stumbled into the street.

Cold air hit her like a brick wall.

Her body felt wrong. It was disconnected, floating, like she wasn't entirely inside herself. The streetlights pulsed in her vision, too bright, too sharp, the world moving too fast.

Somewhere, a horn blared.

Carrie swayed slightly. She needed quiet.

The city moved around her, faceless bodies passing by, coats drawn tight against the wind, their lives continuing as if nothing had changed.

As if everything hadn't just collapsed.

She took a step forward. A bus rumbled in the distance, slowing as it approached the intersection.

The sidewalk was slick with ice, the pavement lined with salt stains. The people around her waited for the pedestrian light, their faces blank, unaware of the storm rising inside her.

Her breath fogged in the air, fast and uneven.

She stepped off the curb. The world tilted.

The bus was closer now, headlights cutting through the icy dusk, its deep mechanical growl reverberating through her chest.

She could end it.

The thought didn't come as a decision but as an inevitability.

She could end it right here, right now, in front of all of them. A clean break. A violent, undeniable end.

No one could ignore that.

She took another step.

The sound of screeching brakes split the air. People screamed. Carrie never heard if she was one of them.

Carrie awoke to the sound of something unknown.

A low, droning hum. Not a melody, not a song, just a noise, constant and pulsing, like the buzzing of a dying light bulb or the flickering static of an old television.

Her eyelids were heavy, crusted at the edges, her mouth thick with the sour taste of something chemical. Her limbs—Jesus, her limbs—felt distant, disconnected, like they belonged to someone else.

And then came a sharp tug at her wrists.

She tried to move, but something held her down.

She gasped, instinct jolting her body into motion, but her arms barely shifted, trapped by the coarse bite of restraints strapped tight across her wrists, across her ankles. The cold leather bit into her skin as she twisted, struggling, her breath coming in fast, shallow pants.

No.

No, no, no.

She bucked against the mattress, her heart slamming into her ribs like a caged animal, her eyes darting wildly around the room, searching, desperate.

White walls. A bolted door. A single flickering light above her, buzzing like a swarm of insects. A camera mounted in the corner, a blinking red dot watching—always watching.

She was in a hospital.

No. Something worse.

A prison.

Carrie let out a sharp, ragged breath, her head lolling to the side, cheek scraping against the stiff cotton of the pillow.

That's when she saw him.

A man stood at the foot of the bed, dressed in a crisp white coat, hands folded over a clipboard, pen poised like a weapon. He was in his late forties, maybe older, with neatly combed dark hair flecked with gray, thin wire-rimmed glasses perched on the bridge of his nose.

His face was unreadable, lips set in a careful line, but his eyes were too focused, too patient.

A man who had seen this all before.

"Miss Langley," the doctor said smoothly, like the words had been practiced, like he had said them a hundred times before to people just like her.

Carrie stared at him, breath still coming in short, rapid bursts. She could hear her pulse pounding in her ears.

"I'm afraid you had an episode," he continued, glancing down at his clipboard, flipping a page. "You were brought in after attempting to harm yourself. Do you remember?"

A flash. Cold air. Headlights cutting through the dusk. A bus. Screeching brakes. Hands pulling her back.

Carrie swallowed, her tongue thick and useless in her mouth.

"I'm not supposed to be here," she croaked, throat raw and scraped from disuse.

The doctor made a note, his expression unreadable.

"You're being held under observation," he continued. "You will remain here until we determine you are stable."

Stable.

The word rattled in her skull, hollow and meaningless.

She let out a short, sharp laugh, the sound gurgling from her throat like smoke.

Stable.

They had strapped her down. They had trapped her here.

Carrie let her head fall back against the pillow, eyes flickering to the ceiling, breath shuddering. Her body ached, muscles weak, drained of whatever fight she had left.

The doctor watched her carefully, pen poised, waiting.

Then, finally, he spoke again.

"Do you remember what happened?"

Carrie stared at the ceiling.

"I remember a woman," she murmured.

The doctor didn't respond, waiting.

"A woman who was supposed to protect them," Carrie continued, her voice light, sing-song, the edges of her lips curling. "But she didn't. She let them slip through her fingers like water, like a current pulling them away. She just stood there."

The pen scratched against the paper.

Carrie turned her head slowly, lips parting, breath slow and deliberate.

"They all think it was an accident, don't they?" she whispered.

The doctor said nothing.

Carrie smiled, wide and sharp, teeth glinting under the artificial light.

"But I know better," she breathed.

The doctor made another note while Carrie let out a slow exhale, fingers twitching against the restraints, body going slack against the mattress.

"She doesn't know," she murmured, voice dropping to something almost conspiratorial. "The mother. She doesn't know what it's like to watch, to see everything so clearly, to understand what must be done."

Her breath hitched.

"I could have saved them."

The doctor glanced up, his gaze sharpening.

Carrie's eyes gleamed, bright and fevered, pupils blown wide.

"I was the only one who could," she whispered.

Another note.

Carrie licked her lips, voice dropping lower, softer, turning into something almost like a lullaby.

"There's always a mother," she murmured. "One who is too blind to see. One who lets them go."

She inhaled deeply, savoring the moment, eyes slipping closed.

"They blame the wrong woman."

The doctor shifted slightly. "Who do you think is to blame, Miss Langley?"

Carrie didn't answer right away. She tilted her head, studying him, eyes flickering with something dark, something unfathomable.

And then, she laughed.

A soft, breathy sound, curling at the edges. It was the kind of laugh that didn't belong in a place like this.

"I think you already know," she murmured.

The doctor hesitated.

Another note.

Carrie turned her gaze back to the ceiling. Her lips moved soundlessly, forming the shape of a name.

But she never said it aloud.

15

PRESENT

The first thing I hear when I wake up is the crackle of police radios.

It takes me a moment to place the sound, to separate the murmur of voices outside from the haze of sleep still clinging to my mind. But as I blink at the ceiling, my chest tightens, and reality slams into me like a freight train.

Noah is still missing. He wasn't at the playground.

I sit up too quickly, my body stiff and sore from where I must have fallen asleep on the couch. My clothes are wrinkled, my skin clammy, my throat dry. I barely remember coming home, only that I screamed at the officers at the park, demanding they do more, look harder, before Dan practically dragged me away, whispering, "Izzy, please."

Now, through the living room window, I see them.

Police officers gathered in groups, speaking in low voices. Their radios crackle intermittently, sharp bursts of static cutting through the cold morning air. The sun has barely risen, casting a weak, pale light over the neighborhood.

And then I see them.

The neighbors. Standing on their porches. Watching. Whispering.

Just like they did seven years ago. Just like after the Lockwoods.

A wave of nausea rolls through me, and I tear myself away from the window, wrapping my arms around myself, as though I can physically hold in the dread trying to break free from my chest.

A sharp knock at the door makes me jump. I don't want to answer it. But I already know I don't have a choice.

Detective Birch stands in the doorway, his expression unreadable.

Behind him, Dan lingers near the base of the stairs, his arms crossed tightly over his chest, his jaw set in a hard line.

"Mrs. Warren," Birch says, stepping inside without waiting for an invitation. "I need to ask you a few more questions."

I swallow, my voice hoarse. "I already told you everything."

Birch ignores that, flipping open his notepad. His tone is sharper than yesterday, more clipped.

"Are you absolutely certain you didn't see or hear anything unusual yesterday?"

I stare at him, my pulse quickening. "I already told you I didn't."

"Nothing at all?" His eyes bore into mine. "No cars parked outside that didn't belong? No strangers walking by? No one watching the house?"

The way he says it makes my skin crawl.

Because I did feel like someone was watching. I felt it days ago, when the wind carried a chill that wasn't from the cold. I felt it when the notes arrived. I felt it when I found the door unlocked in the middle of the night.

But if I tell him that now, after the Lockwood tragedy, after the way he looked at me yesterday, he won't see it as evidence. He'll see it as paranoia.

I clench my fists at my sides, forcing my voice to stay steady. "No. I didn't see anything."

Birch exhales through his nose, scribbling something down. He doesn't look at me when he speaks again.

"You told me yesterday you threw away the notes," he says. "Did you ever tell anyone about them before that?"

Dan shifts beside me, his expression tightening. I feel his suspicion, even though he doesn't say anything.

I shake my head. "Only Claire."

Birch glances up. "Claire?"

"She's my best friend. But she only saw the first one. I didn't show her the second."

Birch cocks his head. "Why's that?"

My skin burns. "I didn't want to worry her."

Birch lets that hang in the air between us, his pen tapping lightly against his notepad.

Then, finally, he nods. "Alright."

But I don't believe he's satisfied.

Another knock at the door makes us all turn.

Claire stands there, bundled in an oversized coat, her dyed blonde curls still damp from a rushed shower. She carries a tray of coffee cups, her brow pinched with concern.

"I brought caffeine," she says lightly, but her smile doesn't reach her eyes.

I step forward automatically, taking one of the cups with unsteady hands.

Claire's gaze flicks to Birch, then to Dan, then back to me. She sees the tension in the air, the way my fingers tremble against the cardboard.

"Izzy." Her voice is softer now. "You okay?"

I shake my head. No. I'm not okay. Noah is gone.

The police are wasting time looking at me. And my neighbors are whispering like they already know how this ends.

Claire steps closer, lowering her voice. "They'll find him," she says. "They will."

I nod mechanically, gripping the coffee as if it's something solid, something real to hold onto. But I don't believe her. Because I know how these stories end.

I've lived it before. And I don't know if I'll survive living it again.

The coffee is warm against my palms, but I can't feel it. Everything seems distant, as if I'm watching this scene unfold from somewhere outside my body.

Detective Birch is still here, standing near the window, flipping through his notepad. But I can tell he's already made up his mind about me. Claire stands beside me, a steady presence, her hand resting lightly on my arm.

And Dan, Dan is pacing. His hands are on his hips, his jaw tight, his movements restless, agitated. The Dan I know is calm, logical, measured. But this Dan, this version of him, is unraveling.

Just like me.

"Can we just stop?" Dan's voice snaps through the tension like a whip. "Can we take a second to breathe before we start jumping to conclusions again?"

I look up at him, my head pounding.

"Jumping to conclusions?" My voice is raw, shaking. "Our son is missing, Dan. What do you think I'm supposed to do? Sit down and have some tea?"

Dan drags a hand through his hair. "That's not what I'm saying—"

"You don't believe me." My throat tightens. "You never believe me."

Dan exhales sharply, like he's trying to hold onto his

patience. "Izzy, listen to yourself. You're running in circles. You say someone took Noah, but you don't know who. You say you got threatening notes, but then you threw them away. And now you're saying this is connected to..." He stops himself, shaking his head.

I clench my fists. "To Theo and Charlotte."

Dan's jaw tightens. "It's not the same."

I let out a hollow laugh, my chest heaving. "Isn't it?"

Dan's face darkens. "No, Izzy. It isn't. This isn't some nightmare from seven years ago. This is real. Right now. And the police are trying to help, but you're not," he rubs his temples. "You're not making any sense."

I flinch.

Claire steps in, her voice gentle but firm. "Dan, that's not fair."

Dan lets out a humorless laugh, turning to her. "Not fair? Claire, listen to her. She's all over the place! I want to believe her, but the way she's acting," he shakes his head, "she looks unstable."

Something inside me cracks.

Claire stiffens beside me, her grip tightening on my arm. "She's scared, Dan."

Dan shakes his head, stepping back, putting space between us. "She's making herself look guilty."

I suck in a sharp breath, my body going rigid.

Guilty.

The word slices through me, sending ice into my veins.

I stare at him, something shifting behind my ribs, something breaking.

"Is that what you think?" My voice is barely above a whisper.

Dan exhales, running both hands over his face. "I don't know what to think, Izzy."

Silence.

I feel it pressing in on me, wrapping around my throat, suffocating me.

Claire steps between us, a protective force, her voice controlled but edged with steel. "This is not helping. Fighting with Izzy isn't going to bring Noah back."

Dan swallows, nodding stiffly, but I see the exhaustion in his eyes, the doubt creeping in like a shadow.

He doesn't know what to do with me anymore. He doesn't trust me. And that realization makes my stomach lurch.

I squeeze my eyes shut, willing my breath to slow. I have to keep it together. I have to. Because I can feel the way Birch watches me like I'm an open case file, the way Dan flinches when I raise my voice.

I know what this looks like. And if I don't pull myself together, I won't just lose Noah. I'll lose everything.

Detective Birch clears his throat, shifting his weight slightly. He looks at me the way you'd look at a shirt with a stain on it, like he's trying to decide if it's worth keeping or throwing away.

"We've circulated a picture of Noah to the news channels."

His words barely register at first, my brain sluggish and slow, still tangled in the argument with Dan. My vision is swimming with images. Noah's small hands grasping the hem of my sweater, his sleepy morning curls, the way he always asks for just one more bedtime story.

And now his face will be everywhere.

On televisions. Like them. Like Theo and Charlotte.

A cold, clammy wave of nausea rolls through me. "What?"

Birch exhales, flipping through his notepad, speaking with the patience of someone explaining something to a child. "We've put out an Amber Alert. Local stations are already running it. His description, his last known whereabouts. Our hope is that if someone has seen him, they'll come forward."

My stomach drops. Noah's gone. And it's real.

People will see his face on the screen. His small, frozen expression staring back at them, and they'll wonder what happened.

And some of them, just like Birch, will think they already know. That I know more than I'm saying. That it's my fault.

I shake my head, gripping the edge of the table, my knuckles white. "This isn't happening."

Dan rubs a hand over his jaw, his face pale, his body rigid. "It's a good thing, Izzy," he says quietly, like he's trying to reason with me. "This will help us find him."

I barely hear him. My skin is too tight, my breath too shallow. "The Lockwood kids."

Birch looks up sharply.

Dan stiffens. "Izzy."

I swallow, my throat dry. "The media, when it was Theo and Charlotte, they," I suck in a sharp breath. "They tore me apart."

Birch's mouth presses into a hard line.

Dan turns to him, his voice careful. "That won't happen here."

Birch doesn't answer immediately. He closes his notepad slowly, watching me. "You were never charged with anything, Mrs. Warren."

I let out a brittle laugh. "That doesn't mean people didn't come to their own conclusions."

Birch's gaze lingers. "And yet, here we are."

Dan exhales sharply, stepping forward. "Look, let's just focus on finding my son, okay?" His voice is firmer now, laced with frustration. "We're wasting time."

Birch doesn't look away from me. "Are we?"

The question lands like a slap.

I go still.

Dan's jaw tightens. "What the hell is that supposed to mean?"

Birch remains unmoving, unreadable. "It means we need to be thorough."

Dan's shoulders bunch. "Are you accusing my wife of something?"

Birch exhales through his nose, carefully measured. "No one's accusing anyone. But we need the full picture."

Dan shakes his head, his voice low, edged with warning. "This isn't about her."

Birch finally looks at him, and something unspoken passes between them. A quiet assessment. A line being drawn.

Dan is still on my side. But he's standing further away now.

I can feel it, the slow shift in his posture, the weight of doubt pressing into him.

I close my eyes for half a second, willing myself to stay calm. Because I know the truth. And I know that the longer I look unstable, the easier it is for them to stop looking for the real threat.

I square my shoulders, forcing my voice to stay even. "What's next?"

Birch watches me for a moment longer, then flips his notepad shut. "We keep searching. We keep questioning people." A pause. "And we wait for something to break."

The words make my skin crawl. Because I know what waiting means.

Waiting is what they did with the Lockwood case. Waiting is what turned me into the story instead of the missing children. Waiting means I lose control of the narrative.

I can't let that happen again.

Dan exhales, rubbing his temples. "And if nothing does?"

Birch gives a small, unreadable smile.

"Something always does."

16

7 YEARS AGO

A week had passed.

The Lockwood estate remained still, eerily untouched by time, as if the tragedy that had unfolded within its walls had been frozen there, preserved in silence. The media had begun to retreat, shifting their attention to fresher scandals and newer victims. Yet, whispers of the case still lingered in the air, like smoke curling into unseen corners.

Evelyn sat in her drawing room, the afternoon light casting long, golden streaks across the polished floor. The house was empty, and silent echoes lived everywhere. The creak of the staircase where Charlotte had once tiptoed at night, the rustling of leaves beyond the window where Theo had played, the imagined hush of small voices now lost to the dark.

She exhaled slowly, rolling the stem of her wine glass between her fingers.

There was only one thing left undone.

She picked up the phone.

Three hours away, in a small town in southern New Hampshire, Isabel sat curled up on the couch, her laptop open in her lap, yet her eyes weren't on the screen. She was staring at the muted television, watching the news ticker crawl across the bottom.

"LOCKWOOD CASE: PUBLIC STILL DIVIDED ON DISMISSED CHARGES"

She exhaled, rubbing her temple.

The months since she had left Maine had been slow and suffocating. The media attention had lessened, but it had not disappeared. She had stayed with her parents in their modest colonial-style home, surrounded by the familiar sound of a life she had left behind long ago. It should have been comforting, should have made her feel safe.

It hadn't.

She still woke in the middle of the night, tangled in her sheets, Evelyn's voice from that last night ringing in her head. Get out of my house.

The phone rang.

Isabel startled, sitting up straighter, glancing at her mother, who stood by the kitchen sink, watching her cautiously.

Her phone continued to ring.

She hesitated before answering. "Hello?"

A pause.

Then "Isabel."

The voice sent an immediate chill down her spine. Evelyn.

Isabel sat frozen, gripping the phone tighter.

"I—" She swallowed. "I wasn't expecting to hear from you."

"I need to see you."

Isabel's pulse spiked. She pressed her free hand into her knee, grounding herself.

"Evelyn, I don't think that's a good idea."

"I just want to talk." There was something eerily calm about her voice. Not angry, not broken. Just steady.

"I don't." Isabel shook her head, forcing herself to stay firm. "Evelyn, the case is closed. I don't know what there is to say."

Evelyn sighed softly on the other end of the line.

"I know. But I still need to see you."

There was a weight to those words, something Isabel couldn't quite place.

Evelyn continued, her voice as smooth as ever. "I understand why you'd be hesitant, which is why I'm suggesting somewhere neutral. Somewhere public."

Public.

Even after all this time, even though she had been cleared, Isabel was still a name that turned heads. People still whispered, still stared too long when she went into town, still speculated whether justice had truly been served.

She could not be seen meeting with Evelyn Lockwood. The press would have a field day.

Still, some part of her hesitated.

Isabel didn't know if it was guilt, grief, or simply the exhaustion of constantly being watched, but something in her faltered.

And Evelyn, as always, knew exactly when to strike.

"I can come to you."

Isabel's stomach clenched.

She didn't want Evelyn here, in this house, in her parents' space but at least it would be controlled. No strangers. No cameras. No prying eyes.

A long pause stretched between them.

Then softly, reluctantly, Isabel exhaled.

"Okay."

~

The road stretched endlessly ahead, winding through the quiet, wooded landscape of southern New Hampshire was starkly different from the sweeping coastal roads of Maine.

The scenery lacked the vastness, the grandeur. No towering cliffs overlooked the gray Atlantic, no sprawling private estates hid behind iron gates. Instead, there were stretches of farmland, clusters of modest homes, and long, empty roads lined with maple trees shedding the last of their brittle autumn leaves.

Mr. Doyle drove in silence, his gloved hands steady on the wheel. The car, a sleek black sedan that looked too expensive for these roads, glided over the asphalt without a sound, a shadow cutting through the small-town quiet.

Evelyn sat in the back, her gaze unfocused, staring out the window. She had not spoken much during the drive.

The Lockwood estate had been suffocating. Too still, too hollow. Every room drained of life, every object untouched since the night it all fell apart.

Oliver was gone more than he was home. The staff moved as if walking through a house of ghosts. And Evelyn could no longer bear the way the walls seemed to whisper when she was alone.

So, she had come here.

Not for closure. For answers.

Isabel watched from the window as the black sedan pulled up outside the modest colonial-style house she had grown up in.

The car looked wrong here. And Evelyn Lockwood looked wrong here.

The house, unlike the Lockwood estate, had no grand columns, no sprawling drive, no perfectly symmetrical façade. The white paint had begun to peel in places, the garden was unruly, the porch let out a slight creak whenever someone stepped on the second plank. It was not a house built for appearances. It was a home. And it was a home that had not known tragedy.

Until now.

Isabel pressed her hands into the worn fabric of the couch, forcing herself to breathe. She had been a fool to agree to this.

A sharp knock on the door.

She stood quickly, wiping her palms against her jeans before making her way to the door. She inhaled sharply, then pulled it open.

There she was.

Evelyn Lockwood stood on the porch, wrapped in a thick cashmere coat, her blonde hair pulled into a sleek twist, her lips pressed into a thin, impenetrable line.

For the first time since Isabel had met her, Evelyn looked out of place.

The wealthy, untouchable woman had stepped into another world where her name carried no weight, where no one would rush to refill her wine glass or straighten the hem of her dress.

For a brief moment, they simply stared at each other.

Then, Evelyn spoke.

"I'm sorry," she said.

It was barely a whisper, but it was there.

Her face crumpled, just for a moment, just long enough for Isabel to glimpse something raw, something human behind the mask. Her hands trembled slightly at her sides, and when she spoke again, her voice was thin.

"I loved them so much."

Isabel's throat tightened. She had not expected this.

months, she had replayed their last conversation. The screaming, the accusations, the way Evelyn had banished her from that house like she had been the one who put the children in the lake.

She had not expected Evelyn Lockwood to come to her door and break.

"Come inside," Isabel murmured before she could stop herself.

Evelyn nodded stiffly and stepped over the threshold.

The women sat in the small living room, cups of tea steaming between them, untouched. The air was thick with unspoken things, the silence stretching long enough that it became a third presence in the room.

Evelyn sat with perfect posture, but it was clear she was uncomfortable. She did not belong in this house among its creaking floorboards, its well-worn furniture, its warmth.

She belonged in a place of marble and ice.

Her gaze swept over the faded floral wallpaper, the family photographs on the mantel, the slight fray at the edge of the couch cushion.

This was not the kind of house where children drowned in lakes. Not the kind of house where mothers failed their children.

"I don't think you killed my children, Isabel."

The words were spoken softly, but they sliced through the room like a blade.

Isabel inhaled sharply, her fingers tightening around the delicate porcelain of the teacup.

Evelyn's blue eyes met hers. Steady, assessing.

"But I also don't believe you protected them."

A breath. A beat.

The words landed between them like a funeral bell.

Evelyn watched for a reaction, but Isabel didn't speak. Because what could she say? What could she possibly say that Evelyn would believe?

"I should have been there."

Evelyn's voice wavered slightly, just enough to crack the mask she had spent months reconstructing.

"I should have," She stopped, swallowed, then set her cup down with measured grace.

She would not cry again. Not here. Not in this house that did not belong to her.

The warmth of the tea filled the air between them, thin wisps of steam rising and vanishing.

Then Evelyn leaned forward slightly, folding her hands in her lap, her gaze turning cold again, sharp again.

"You need to leave," she said simply.

Isabel blinked, her stomach tightening.

"This town will never forgive and forget," Evelyn continued, her voice barely above a whisper. "And neither will I."

The words sent a chill down Isabel's spine.

Evelyn held her gaze for another long moment, then smoothed down the front of her coat, rose to her feet, and walked toward the door.

Isabel did not stop her.

She listened as the door opened, and closed again, and as the sedan rumbled to life.

Then, just like that she was gone.

The house felt heavier after Evelyn left, as if she had taken the air with her and left only the weight of her words behind.

Isabel sat motionless for a long time, her fingers still curled around the cooling porcelain of her untouched tea. The silence pressed against her ears, broken only by the distant roar of an engine retreating down the street.

She had known, deep down, that this was coming.

Evelyn had never been the type to let things lie.

She had come here not just to say what needed to be said, but to remind Isabel of something she already knew.

That she could never stay.

Slowly, mechanically, Isabel set her cup down and reached for the phone.

It rang twice before a familiar voice answered.

"Linda?" Isabel's voice came out thinner than she expected.

A pause, then a warm, cautious reply. "Isabel? It's been a while."

"I know," Isabel exhaled. "I," she hesitated, squeezing her eyes shut. "I need a place to go for a few days. Just to clear my head."

Linda, her old college roommate, was silent for a moment. "Where are you now?"

"New Hampshire. My parents' place."

"That's… far," Linda murmured. "Are you okay?"

"No." Isabel shook her head, though Lucy couldn't see her. "But I will be. I just need some space. I won't be in the way."

"Don't be ridiculous. Of course, you can stay." Linda's voice softened. "Come to Richmond. We'll figure it out."

Relief washed over Isabel like a wave. "Thank you."

Linda hesitated again. "You know they're still talking about you, right?"

"I know." Isabel swallowed. "That's why I need to leave."

While Evelyn sat in the back of the sedan, her body remained still, hands clasped tightly in her lap as the car cut through the rural landscape. The hum of the tires against the road was rhythmic, almost hypnotic, but her thoughts were anything but settled.

She had done what she came to do. She had warned Isabel. Told her to leave.

So why did it still feel like something was left undone?

The day the children died had begun like any other. She had gone to her tennis lesson, as always. The air had been crisp, the morning sun bright against the court. She had spent hours perfecting her backhand, letting the rhythm of the game drown out the noise in her head.

And then the call had come.

Even now, she could hear the way Mr. Doyle's voice had

cracked on the other end of the line. The way time had stopped the moment she heard the words: There's been an accident.

She had rushed home. But it was already too late.

She pressed a hand to her temple, letting out a long slow breath.

It had been months. The case was closed. The coroner's report had confirmed the obvious drowning. No foul play. No signs of trauma. A tragic accident, nothing more.

And yet.

Something in her refused to rest. A gnawing, uneasy feeling that something was off, that the truth had slipped through the cracks, lost in the frenzy of grief and blame.

She had been too broken to dig deeper. Too drained to investigate. She had let the world focus its anger on Isabel because it was easier than facing the possibility that something far worse had happened.

But now, Isabel was gone. And for the first time, Evelyn had to sit with what remained.

She closed her eyes as the car sped along the darkening road.

She had told Isabel to leave.

But Evelyn Lockwood was not a woman who let things go forever.

She had let Isabel slip away for now.

But one day, perhaps when Isabel least expected it, Evelyn would return. And she would get the truth. And have her revenge.

One way or another.

17

PRESENT

The house is too quiet.

It's the kind of silence that doesn't soothe, doesn't settle. It presses down like a weight, thick and suffocating and filling the spaces where Noah's laughter should be.

I've spent the entire day answering the same questions over and over, watching officers come and go, watching Dan's face change and his frustration growing, his patience thinning.

Now, the only sound is the ticking of the clock.

Tick.

Tick.

Tick.

Dan and I lie in bed, both facing opposite directions, our bodies stiff, restless. Neither of us has spoken in what feels like hours, but I can hear his shallow breathing, the way his body shifts every few minutes, the tension coiled in his muscles.

Neither of us will sleep.

Not without Noah here.

I close my eyes, pressing my hands against my face, trying to will away the images flashing through my mind of the empty yard, the cold wind, the sickening realization that I had only turned away for a second, and somehow, that had been long enough.

The gut-twisting certainty that this is happening again.

I exhale shakily, forcing myself to focus on the sheets beneath my fingertips, the slow rise and fall of my own chest.

And then the phone rings.

I bolt upright.

Dan stirs beside me, groggy, confused. "What the—"

I don't wait. I don't think. I throw off the blankets and scramble toward the nightstand, snatching up my phone with shaking fingers.

A number I don't recognize.

But somehow, I know.

I press the phone to my ear.

"Hello?" My voice is breathless, desperate.

For a moment, there's nothing. Just static.

Then a child's voice, soft and distant.

"Mommy?"

The sound slices through me like a blade, sending ice through my veins. My breath catches, my grip on the phone tightening so hard my knuckles turn white.

"Noah?" I gasp. "Noah, baby, is that you?"

Silence.

Then, a soft exhale so faint, I almost think I imagined it.

I clutch the phone with both hands, my entire body trembling. "*Noah, please, where are you?*"

Nothing.

The line goes dead.

A strangled, guttural sound rips from my throat. "No!"

Dan is fully awake now, sitting up, his face pale and drawn. "Izzy, what the hell?"

I'm already dialing the number back, my fingers moving too fast, slipping against the screen.

It rings. And rings. And rings.

"The number you have dialed is no longer in service."

I stare at the screen, my breath coming in sharp, broken gasps. This isn't real. This can't be real.

Dan swings his legs over the side of the bed, rubbing his hands over his face. "Izzy, what happened?"

I can barely get the words out. "It was him." My voice breaks. "It was Noah."

Dan's expression hardens. "What?"

I clutch my stomach, my body swaying. "He, he said, 'Mommy.'"

Dan is on his feet now, grabbing the phone from my hands, checking the screen. His frown deepens. "Who called?"

I shake my head, my pulse erratic. "I don't know, I, I didn't recognize the number, but then it was disconnected, and," I choke on a sob, my fingers digging into my scalp. "Dan, it was him. I know it was him."

Dan exhales sharply, his face pinched with exhaustion, frustration. "Izzy."

"I know my son's voice."

He drags a hand down his face, his shoulders slumping. "It's the middle of the night, you're exhausted, and"

My eyes fix his. "You think I imagined it?"

Dan doesn't answer right away.

And that hesitation, that half-second pause, is all I need to know.

I stagger back, shaking my head violently. "No."

"Izzy."

"No." My voice is hoarse, breaking. "I'm not crazy."

"I didn't say you were."

"But you think it."

Dan sighs heavily, raking a hand through his hair. "Izzy, this doesn't make sense. If someone took him, why would they have him call you?"

I don't know. I don't have a goddamn clue. All I know is that I heard my son. And he's out there somewhere.

I don't think. I just move. Barefoot and shaking, I hurry down the stairs, my breath still caught somewhere between a gasp and a sob. The house is dark, the only light spilling in from the streetlamps outside.

Through the window, I see the patrol car parked at the curb, its headlights dimmed in a silent presence in the night.

I yank open the front door, stepping onto the porch, the cold air biting against my skin.

Officer Jordan looks up from where she stands near the car, her breath curling in the chilly night air. She's tall, with strong shoulders and an athletic build, her dark brown skin illuminated by the glow of the porch light. Her black hair is pulled into neat, tight braids that fall just past her collar, and her uniform is crisp, her stance steady and capable.

She's been stationed outside since earlier this evening, a presence meant to reassure me. But right now, all I feel is panic clawing at my chest.

She straightens immediately at the sight of me, her sharp eyes narrowing. "Mrs. Warren? What's wrong?"

I wrap my arms around myself, trying to keep my voice steady. "I just got a phone call." My throat tightens. "It was him."

Her expression grows serious. "Who?"

"Noah." My voice is barely a whisper. "I heard him. He said, Mommy."

Jordan steps forward, the professionalism in her face shifting into something more urgent. "You're sure it was him?"

I nod frantically. "I know my son's voice." I clutch my arms tighter, my breath coming in sharp bursts. "The number was unknown, but when I called back, it was disconnected."

She mutters something under her breath, already pulling out her radio. "I need you to stay here, inside the house. I'll alert Detective Birch and see if we can trace the call."

I barely hear her. My pulse pounds in my ears.

She watches me for a second longer, then softens. "Mrs. Warren, I know this is terrifying. But if someone called you, that means Noah is alive."

The words should be comforting.

But all I can think is, for how long?

I swallow hard, nodding stiffly, and step back inside. I close the door with shaking fingers, pressing my back against it. My whole body feels unsteady, like I might collapse under the weight of it all.

And then, a knock.

I whip the door open.

Claire stands there, holding coffee, her face full of concern.

"I figured you wouldn't sleep," she says.

I exhale, pressing a hand to my forehead.

Claire steps closer, lowering her voice. "Izzy, what happened?"

I don't answer. I can't. Because for the first time, I realize whoever took Noah, whoever left the notes, whoever called me, they aren't just trying to scare me. They're playing with me. They're punishing me.

Claire steps inside without hesitation, shutting the door behind her. The scent of coffee and her subtle vanilla perfume follows her in, but nothing feels comforting right now. Nothing feels safe.

She hands me one of the cups, and I take it with shaking hands, but I don't drink. I don't trust myself to.

"Izzy." Her voice is soft but steady. "Tell me what happened."

I shake my head, gripping the cup tighter. "The call." My voice cracks. "It was him, Claire. It was Noah."

She freezes. "You're sure?"

I nod frantically, the weight of it pressing into my chest like a cinder block. "He said Mommy." I swallow hard. "And then the line went dead."

Claire exhales slowly, setting her coffee down on the table. "Did the police trace it?"

"They're trying," I murmur. "But I, I don't think they believe me."

Claire's brows knit together. "Of course they do. They're here, they're looking."

I let out a sharp, humorless laugh. "No, Claire. They're watching me."

She frowns. "What do you mean?"

I lift my gaze to hers, my chest rising and falling in uneven bursts. "Because of before."

She tilts her head slightly. "Before?"

I don't know why I hesitate. Maybe because I've never told her this story. Maybe because I swore I never would.

But now, the words are clawing their way out of me. And I let them.

I set my coffee down with trembling hands and move toward the couch. Claire follows, sitting beside me, watching me carefully. I press my palms against my knees, trying to steady myself.

And then I say their names.

"Theo and Charlotte Lockwood."

Claire watches me, her expression unreadable. "Who are they?"

I inhale shakily. "I was their nanny."

She blinks, surprised.

"I was twenty-five when I started working for the Lockwoods," I continue, my voice quieter now. "They were this... picture-perfect family. A beautiful house. Money. Influence."

I shake my head. "But beneath it? They were so broken."

Claire says nothing, just listens.

"Their father, Oliver, was charming but absent. The kind of man who could make you feel like the center of his world one second and then like you never existed the next. Their mother, Evelyn, was distant. Cold."

I stare at my hands, my voice barely above a whisper.

"And then there were the kids. Theo and Charlotte."

The memories crash into me like a wave.

"Theo was five. Smart, sensitive. He had this way of looking at you, like he already understood things far beyond his years." A lump forms in my throat, but I push forward.

"And Charlotte... she was three. Just like Noah."

Claire's breath hitches, but she doesn't interrupt.

I squeeze my hands together. "She was wild. A little firecracker. She loved running barefoot in the grass, loved splashing in puddles, loved... everything. She had the biggest laugh, the kind that made you laugh just by hearing it."

I close my eyes. "I loved them. God, I loved them."

The silence that follows is unbearable.

And then, I say it.

"The day they died... it was supposed to be a normal day." My voice is so small now, so fragile. "They were playing by the lake while I packed up their toys. Just seconds, Claire. I turned away for seconds." My breath shudders. "And when I looked back... they were gone."

Claire sucks in a sharp breath. "Oh my God."

I feel my nails digging into my palms. "I ran. I searched everywhere. I screamed their names so loudly my throat felt raw." A tear slips down my cheek, but I don't wipe it away.

"Then I saw it. The water. It was too still."

I shut my eyes tightly, willing the images away.

"They found their bodies later," I whisper. "They said it was an accident. That children wander, that water is dangerous, that I should have been watching."

I let out a hollow breath. "But Evelyn didn't believe that. She blamed me. She told the world that I had failed her children."

Claire shakes her head, horrified. "Jesus, Izzy."

"The media ripped me apart," I say bitterly. "The trial was public. My face was everywhere. And even though I was cleared, even though they never proved I was at fault... it didn't matter."

I look up at her, my vision blurry. "Because people had already decided I was guilty."

Claire is silent for a long time.

Then, finally, she whispers, "I had no idea."

I nod, swallowing the lump in my throat. "And now, Noah is gone. And the police," I shake my head. "They remember me. Birch remembers me." My chest tightens. "And I know what that means. Instead of looking for my son, they're looking at me."

Claire's face darkens. "That's bullshit."

A bitter laugh escapes me. "Is it?"

She grips my hands suddenly, squeezing them tight. "Izzy, listen to me. You did not take Noah. You did not take those kids."

Her eyes are fierce, unwavering. "And I swear to you, we are going to find your son. We are going to prove them wrong."

Her words press into my skin, into my bones.

I nod because I want to believe her. I need to believe her. But in the back of my mind, a horrible thought lingers.

What if Noah was taken by someone who already knows all of this? Someone who has been waiting. Watching. Someone who knows exactly how to make me look guilty all over again.

A shiver rolls down my spine, an intrusive thought creeping into the edges of my mind, whispering something so awful, so impossible, that I almost shake it away.

Almost. But it lingers.

I pull back from Claire slightly, my pulse stuttering as the name forms in my mind—sharp and deliberate.

Evelyn Lockwood.

I swallow hard, my mouth suddenly dry.

Could it be her? Would she, could she, do something like this?

I think of the last time I saw her. Her face was pale, hollow, her sharp blue eyes burning into me with something more than grief. With blame.

"You didn't protect them."

Her voice echoes in my head, a ghost from seven years ago.

I look at Claire, my throat tightening. "What if," I hesitate, my voice barely above a whisper. "What if it's her?"

Claire frowns. "Who?"

I wet my lips, forcing myself to say it.

"Evelyn Lockwood."

Claire blinks, clearly taken aback. "The kids mother?"

I nod stiffly, gripping the coffee cup tighter. "She hated me, Claire. She blamed me for everything. She wanted me to suffer." I exhale shakily. "What if this is her way of making me feel what she felt?"

Claire's brows knit together, her lips parting slightly but she doesn't speak. Because she knows it's not impossible. Because if Evelyn Lockwood wanted revenge, what better way to destroy me than to take my son?

18

3 YEARS AGO

The walls of St. Jude Psychiatric Facility had always felt too white. Too clean. Too hollow. For four years, Carrie Langley had lived within them, moving through the same routines, eating the same meals at the same tables, enduring the same blank stares from the same doctors who thought they understood her.

And for four years, she had learned patience.

She had come and gone, in and out, released on good behavior, only to return when the weight of her mind became too much to bear. There were nights she had screamed until her throat was raw, clawed at her own arms, whispered to shadows no one else could see. They had sedated her, restrained her, forced her into cold showers, and locked her away in small, dark rooms where time ceased to exist. And each time, she had let them believe she was breaking.

Because pity was a currency. And she had spent it wisely.

Now, it was time.

She sat in the common room, the morning light filtering through barred windows, painting thin golden streaks across the linoleum floor. In her hands, she held the discharge papers freshly signed, still crisp at the edges. Her fingers traced the letters of her own name, written in smooth, steady strokes. Not shaky. Not hesitant. Stable.

Dr. Hewitt sat across from her, his gray eyes watching her carefully over the rim of his glasses. He had been with her from the beginning, through the breakdowns, the relapses, the whispered confessions of regret. He had seen her at her worst.

And now, he saw her at her best.

"I'm glad to see you doing so well, Carrie," he said, folding his hands in his lap. "Your progress has been remarkable."

She smiled, soft, grateful and reformed. "Thank you, Doctor. I couldn't have done it without all of you."

He nodded, satisfied. "Do you have somewhere to go?"

"Yes," she lied. "A friend is expecting me."

"Good." He exhaled, reaching for the call button to summon an orderly. "Remember what we talked about. Take things slow. Build a life for yourself outside of all this."

Carrie nodded, her smile never faltering. "Of course."

A nurse arrived, carrying a neatly packed bag of her belongings. Nothing much, just a few clothes, a notebook, a cheap paperback novel she had never finished. They walked her to the front desk, where the final papers were stamped, the last signatures scrawled in bureaucratic ink.

Then, just like that, she was free.

The air outside felt different. Lighter. Colder. Real.

Carrie stood on the sidewalk, adjusting to the absence of walls around her. The facility loomed behind her, its gates locked, its windows high and narrow, keeping the lost ones inside. But she was no longer lost. She had found clarity.

She had found purpose.

There had been times over the last four years when she thought she might never leave. When the darkness had eaten at her from the inside out, when she had stared at herself in the mirror and seen nothing but an empty shell. But Carrie was not empty. No, she was full of knowledge, full of patience, full of something deeper, something sharper, something the doctors could never quite reach.

She had spent years convincing them she was better. That she was healed.

She turned her face toward the morning sun, letting it warm her skin. Then, slowly, she smiled.

Her plan could finally begin.

19

PRESENT

Morning comes, but it brings no relief.

The world outside moves forward, just as it always does. Cars passing, birds singing, neighbors walking their dogs. But inside this house, inside me, everything remains frozen.

Noah is still gone.

I barely slept. I drifted in and out, jolting awake at every sound, a car outside, a movement from the officers stationed at the house, a whisper of wind against the window. Each time, I thought this is it. This is the call, the knock on the door.

But it never came.

I pace the living room, arms wrapped around myself, breath shallow. The house is too quiet, too still, the air thick with something heavy and unbearable. Every few minutes, I check my phone, fingers twitching with the urge to call the police again.

Instead, I turn to the officer near the doorway.

Officer Jordan looks up as I approach, her dark eyes steady but unreadable.

"Any news?" My voice is hoarse, barely a whisper.

Her expression softens, but her answer is the same as it's been for the past twenty-four hours.

"Not yet."

I inhale sharply, pressing a hand to my stomach to fight the nausea. "What about the footage? Did they find anything on the traffic cameras? The doorbells? Anything?"

Jordan shakes her head, and I see pity.

"We're working on it, Mrs. Warren."

I hate that answer. I hate that we're doing our best expression. Because it's not enough.

I spin away from her, my head pounding, chest tightening.

I need to do something. I need to get out of this house, to move, to find him. But every road I try to run down is blocked by the police, by Dan, by logic.

And what if I leave and something happens? What if I miss the call? What if...

I stop myself before my thoughts can spiral further. I need to breathe.

I need Noah.

My feet move before I realize it, carrying me up the stairs. I push open his bedroom door and step inside.

His scent still lingers in the air. Baby shampoo and something sweet, something *uniquely him.*

I swallow hard, my hands trembling as I press them against his blankets, fingers curling into the fabric.

Then, slowly, I sink onto his small bed.

His pillow is soft beneath my cheek, and for a second, I can almost trick myself into believing he's just downstairs, that at any moment, he'll run into the room, giggling, asking for his favorite bedtime story.

I pull his blanket up around me, burying my face in its warmth, inhaling deep.

His stuffed lion, worn from too many hugs, lies beside his

pillow. I clutch it to my chest, gripping it so tightly my knuckles ache.

I squeeze my eyes shut.

"Where are you, baby?" My voice is barely a whisper, cracking under the weight of the question.

I don't get an answer.

Just silence.

Just the unbearable, suffocating weight of waiting.

I curl tighter into the bed, gripping his toys, his blankets the last pieces of him I have.

And I wait. Because there's nothing else I can do.

The bed dips slightly.

I don't lift my head.

I don't move at all.

I hear him breathing before he speaks. I hear the soft, shaky inhales, the way he's trying to hold himself together but failing.

Dan.

His hand presses against the blanket near mine. Not touching. Just there. A silent offering. A need for something solid to hold onto.

I swallow hard, my throat aching from all the screaming, all the crying, all the praying that this isn't real. That at any second, we'll wake up, and Noah will be padding down the hallway in his dinosaur pajamas, rubbing sleep from his eyes, asking for breakfast.

But we won't wake up. Because this *is real*. And we are living it.

I shift slightly, just enough to glance up at him.

Dan looks hollow. Like someone has taken a piece of him and left only the shell behind. His skin is pale, his eyes bloodshot, his shoulders slumped as if he's physically carrying the weight of this.

He's holding one of Noah's small socks in his hands, rolling the fabric between his fingers, jaw tight.

Then, suddenly, his face crumbles.

A strangled sob rips from his throat. His entire body shakes as he drops his head into his hands, fingers tangling in his hair.

I stiffen.

Dan doesn't cry.

Not like this.

Not ever.

But now he is breaking apart, coming undone in a way I have never seen before. And I don't know what to do.

"Dan..." My voice is hoarse, cracking under the weight of his grief.

He shakes his head violently, sucking in a gasping breath. "I can't." His voice breaks. "I don't...what if we never see him again?"

I inhale and my stomach lurches. "Don't. Don't say that."

But he's already spiraling, his hands gripping his hair, shoulders trembling. "It's been a day, Izzy. A whole goddamn day. And we don't know anything." He lets out a choked sob, his body collapsing inward. "What if we never, " He stops himself, squeezing his eyes shut. "I can't. I can't lose him."

I push myself up, reaching for him on instinct, my fingers brushing his arm.

He flinches.

I freeze. And something inside me breaks.

"Dan," I whisper. "Look at me."

He shakes his head, his face buried in his hands. "I don't know how to do this." His voice is small, shattered.

Tears blur my vision, thick and suffocating. "Me neither."

He lets out another ragged sob, his breath hitching. "I'm so scared."

My chest tightens so painfully I can barely breathe. I don't know how to fix this. I don't know how to hold him through this kind of pain when I'm drowning in it, too.

So, I do the only thing I can.

I wrap my arms around him. I pull him against me, his body heavy with grief, his fingers gripping the back of my shirt like he's holding onto me for dear life.

We don't speak. We just cry.

Together.

Because Noah is gone, and we don't know how to exist without him.

The hours drag. Each second stretches into eternity, every moment weighed down by the crushing silence of the house.

The officers outside change shifts, their presence steady and unrelenting, but their faces blur together. Their radio chatter hums in the background—empty and meaningless.

Inside, Dan barely speaks.

After breaking down in Noah's room, he retreated into himself, curling up on the couch in the living room, staring blankly at the muted TV. He doesn't acknowledge me when I pass by, doesn't react when I whisper his name.

I understand. Because I feel it too. The house is suffocating me. The walls press closer, the air thick and stale. Every room is a monument to Noah. His toys, his little socks, the crumpled pajamas he left on the floor. His presence is everywhere, but he's nowhere.

I need to get out. I need air.

I grab my phone and press call before I can second-guess myself.

Claire answers on the first ring. "Izzy?"

I inhale shakily. "I need to get out of here."

She doesn't hesitate. "Where are we going?"

I exhale, rubbing my forehead. "I don't know. I just," I swallow. "I feel like I'm suffocating."

Claire hums softly, thinking. "Come meet me at the playground. The one Noah loves."

My stomach clenches. The playground.

I hesitate, gripping the phone tighter. "Claire."

"Izzy," she interrupts gently, "just meet me there. We'll sit, we'll talk. You need fresh air, and you need to breathe."

I shut my eyes, pressing a palm against the counter. The idea of going there, the last place I should be, feels unbearable.

But staying here? Staring at walls that whisper Noah's name? I can't do it anymore.

I inhale deeply, nodding even though she can't see me. "Okay."

Claire's voice softens. "I'll be there in ten."

I hang up, grab my coat, and slip on my shoes with unsteady hands. I glance toward Dan.

He hasn't moved. His face is slack, his eyes empty, his hands clasped in his lap.

"Dan," I say softly.

Nothing.

I step closer, touching his arm gently. "I need to get out for a bit."

His eyes flick toward me, slow and unfocused.

"Claire's meeting me at the playground," I explain hesitantly. "I just need some air."

Dan doesn't react at first. Then, he exhales, running a hand down his face. "Okay."

I hesitate. "Will you be okay?"

He nods, but it's distant. Hollow. "Yeah."

I watch him a moment longer before grabbing my keys and stepping outside.

The wind bites at my cheeks, crisp and cool, as I walk to my car.

I slide into the driver's seat, my breath coming short and shallow.

I don't know if I'm making a mistake. I don't know if I can handle what I'm about to do. But I do know this. If I stay inside that house a second longer, I will fall apart completely.

I turn the key in the ignition and drive.

The playground looms ahead, wrapped in the quiet hush of the late afternoon fog. The air is damp, thick with the scent of wet leaves and earth with the kind of heaviness that clings to your skin.

The world looks muted in this light, gray, blurred at the edges. The swings sway gently in the breeze, empty. A few children play on the jungle gym, their laughter distant, muffled by the mist.

Claire stands near the entrance, her blonde curls tucked into the collar of her coat, hands wrapped around a takeaway coffee cup. She spots me immediately and waves.

I step out of the car, pulling my coat tighter around me. The fog curls around my ankles as I make my way toward her.

"You made it," she says, her voice warm, but there's something unreadable in her eyes.

I nod, swallowing past the lump in my throat. "I needed to get out."

Claire watches me carefully. "I know."

We start walking slow, unhurried. The gravel path crunches beneath our feet.

For the first time in what feels like days, I take a breath that doesn't suffocate me. The air is cold but sharp, cutting through the fog in my brain, momentarily clearing the static.

Neither of us speaks. Claire just walks beside me, sipping her coffee, letting me settle into the moment. Then, as we round a bend in the path, I see it.

Her.

Claire has stopped walking.

She stands still, her eyes locked on the playground.

I follow her gaze.

A group of children is gathered by the slide, their voices soft, their small bodies darting through the mist like ghosts.

Claire watches them with an intensity that sends an unexpected shiver down my spine.

Her lips are slightly parted, her fingers twitching at her side.

Something about the way she looks at them so still, so focused, makes my stomach twist.

"Claire?"

She blinks, snapping out of it, and when she turns back to me, her face is all warmth again, her easy smile sliding into place like it never left.

"You look exhausted, Isabel," she says softly. "Maybe you should get some rest."

I let out a hollow laugh, running a hand over my face. "I don't think I remember how to sleep anymore."

She smiles, but it doesn't quite reach her eyes. "You should try."

I study her for a moment, something unsettled twisting in my gut.

I shake it off. She's just worried about me. That's all.

I force a small smile in return. "Maybe."

The wind rustles through the trees, sending a chill up my spine. And suddenly, I feel it again. That sense.

Someone is watching me.

But this time, it's not the police. And it's not the neighbors.

I glance around the park, my breath quickening. The children keep playing, unaware. The fog clings to the ground, unmoving.

There's no one else. No one at all.

Except Claire. Standing beside me. Watching.

The fog thickens as we walk, curling around the playground like a ghostly veil. The laughter of the children drifts through the damp air, too distant, too faint.

I keep my arms wrapped around myself, the cold seeping into my bones. But I don't think it's the weather.

Claire's voice is soft when she speaks. "Do you ever think about who was really to blame?"

I slow my steps, glancing at her. "What?"

She doesn't look at me. She keeps her eyes forward, still sipping her coffee, as though this is just a casual conversation. As though she's asking about something far less heavy. Far less dark.

"For what happened back then," she clarifies. "To Theo and Charlotte. Do you ever think about who was truly responsible?"

I stare at her, caught off guard. No one has ever asked me that before.

People have assumed the answer. They've already decided it was me. But Claire is asking. Not accusing. Not assuming.

I suck in a breath, my fingers tightening around the sleeves of my coat. "I used to blame myself," I admit. "And maybe, in some ways, I still do. I was their nanny. I should have been watching more closely." My voice wavers, but I force myself to keep going. "But if I had to name someone else?"

Claire nods slightly, encouraging me.

I breathe out, my breath visible in the crisp air. "Oliver."

At the mention of his name, something in my stomach clenches.

Claire finally looks at me, her expression unreadable. "Oliver Lockwood?"

I nod stiffly, my jaw tightening. "It was his fault. He was a scoundrel—he slept with any woman who batted her eyelashes at him, spent more time in hotel rooms than in his own home." I shake my head, anger rising in my chest. "He was never around.

He had this picture-perfect life, a beautiful wife, two perfect children, but he didn't care. He left them alone too much, ignored them unless they were performing for guests, playing the part of the doting father when it suited him." My throat tightens. "His neglect, his absence. That's why Theo and Charlotte are gone."

Claire watches me carefully, sipping her coffee. The silence between us stretches, thick and weighted.

Then, she tilts her head slightly. "And Evelyn?"

I let out a sharp breath. "She blamed me. She had to. It was easier than blaming him. But deep down, she knew."

Claire considers my words. "She never forgave you."

It isn't a question.

I shake my head. "She never will."

Claire's lips curve into a small, knowing smile. "It's funny, isn't it? How grief makes people pick their villains."

Something in her tone makes my spine go rigid. The words settle uncomfortably in my chest, heavy with an understanding that feels too precise, too pointed.

I study her face, searching for some hint of what she's really thinking. But her expression is calm, her posture relaxed.

And yet, for the first time since Noah went missing, a cold prickle crawls up my spine.

And I don't know why.

20

7 YEARS AGO

I left my parents' house before dawn.

I had spent the night listening to the creaking of the old pipes, the distant buzz of my mother's television, and the muffled argument between my parents downstairs that had started the moment I walked through their door.

Evelyn Lockwood had visited me that evening.

She arrived unannounced, stepping into my childhood home as if she belonged there. My mother, never one for confrontation, allowed her in without question, her face drawn with apprehension. My father sat rigidly in his armchair, watching as Evelyn crossed the room, her gaze never leaving mine.

She wasn't cruel. Not exactly. She didn't hurl accusations like Oliver had, nor scream at me like the reporters outside the courtroom. No, her words were measured, careful, like a woman who had spent too much time rehearsing them in her head.

"I don't think you killed my children, Isabel. But I also don't believe you protected them."

That single sentence shattered the last of my composure.

I don't remember what I said in response. I don't even

remember when she left. All I recall is my mother's hands fluttering uselessly at my shoulders, my father's angry muttering about "stirring up trouble," and the suffocating realization that there was nowhere left for me to go.

The town, the house, had become a tomb. I had to leave before it buried me entirely.

So, before dawn, I packed a bag. I took only what I could carry: a few clothes, my identification, and the remains of my savings. I didn't leave a note. My parents would understand why soon enough.

As the sky turned the soft gray of morning, I slipped out of the house and into the unknown.

I ended up in Richmond, Virginia.

I hadn't planned it. I had simply driven until exhaustion forced me to stop, until the road signs became unfamiliar, until I no longer recognized the streets or the people walking them.

I called the only person I could think of. Linda.

Linda and I had been friends in college before life took us in different directions. She had been an artist, a dreamer, someone who lived for late-night conversations and wild ideas. We had lost touch over the years, but when I dialed her number, she picked up on the second ring.

Her voice was the same smoky and warm, tinged with that ever-present curiosity.

She didn't ask questions, just told me to come.

Linda lived in a tiny apartment above a coffee shop, the kind of place that smelled like burnt espresso and oil paints. When I arrived at her doorstep, she took one look at me and pulled me into a fierce hug.

"You look like hell," she murmured against my hair.

"I feel worse."

She let me in.

For the next few weeks, I lived in a strange limbo. Linda gave me space, never pressing for details, never asking why I had shown up at her door with haunted eyes and a past I refused to explain.

I spent my days walking the city, trying to lose myself in the anonymity of the crowds. But no matter how far I went, the past clung to me like a shadow.

Every time I passed a newsstand, my stomach twisted with the irrational fear that my face would be staring back at me from the front page. When people glanced at me on the street, my pulse spiked, convinced they recognized me—that they knew who I was and what I had been accused of.

Linda noticed.

One night, as we sat on her fire escape, watching the city lights flicker against the dark, she finally spoke.

"You can't live like this forever, Izzy."

I flinched at the name. I had told her to call me that—to erase Isabel, to start over.

"I don't have a choice."

"That's bullshit." She exhaled smoke into the night air. "You're free now. No one's looking for you. No one's stopping you from making a life here."

A life.

The words felt foreign. Unreal.

But the idea burrowed into my mind, settling deep in the space where fear had lived for so long.

Maybe Linda was right. Maybe I could build something new.

I found a job at a small independent bookstore.

It wasn't glamorous, but it was safe. The owner, Mrs. Parker, was a sharp-eyed woman in her seventies who had no patience for nonsense. She hired me on the spot, not because I had experience, but because I stacked a pile of books faster than her last employee.

"Just don't be late," she said, handing me an apron.

The work was steady, shelving books, sorting through orders, chatting with customers who lingered too long over poetry collections. The quiet routine soothed something restless inside me.

For the first time in months, I felt like I had control over something.

The fear didn't disappear overnight. It lingered at the edges of my mind, in the way I avoided cameras, in the way my stomach twisted every time someone asked where I was from. But day by day, it grew quieter.

Richmond wasn't home, but it was something close.

It was late spring when he walked into the bookstore.

The air smelled of fresh rain and warm pavement, and the afternoon light slanted golden through the tall windows.

I was at the counter, half-listening to the old jazz record playing in the background when the door swung open and he walked in.

He was tall, broad-shouldered, with a rumpled button-down and the kind of hair that looked like he constantly ran his hands through it. He had a presence—something steady, something that made the air shift around him.

He wandered through the aisles with an easy familiarity, pausing now and then to run his fingers along the spines of books.

I should have ignored him. I usually did. But something about him made me pause.

"You look lost," I said before I could stop myself.

He glanced up, his eyes warm and sharp all at once. "Maybe. Or maybe I just like the way bookstores smell on rainy days."

I smirked despite myself. "That's a terrible reason to buy a book."

"It's a great reason to pretend I'm looking," he countered.

I tilted my head. "Then what do you really want?"

Something flickered across his expression—something unreadable. Then, just as quickly, he grinned.

"A recommendation," he said. "Something I wouldn't normally pick up."

I hesitated. Then, without thinking, I reached for Rebecca.

He read the title, one brow arching. "A gothic mystery?"

"It's about a woman who can't escape the past," I said.

The words hung between us, heavier than I intended.

Something in his gaze sharpened, like he had caught on to something unspoken. But instead of pressing, he smiled.

"Sounds like my kind of story."

I rang up the book. He lingered by the counter, his fingers tapping lightly against the cover.

"I'll let you know what I think," he said before walking out the door.

And just like that, Daniel Warren stepped into my life. I didn't know it yet, but that moment would change everything.

Richmond was never meant to be permanent.

I had arrived with no real plan, only the desperate need to disappear, to carve out a space where the past couldn't reach me. At first, I told myself I was only passing through. A month, maybe two. Just long enough to catch my breath before moving on.

But life has a strange way of shifting beneath your feet when you least expect it.

Days blurred into weeks. Weeks into months. And before I knew it, I wasn't just surviving anymore, I was living.

Mrs. Parker ran her store like a tiny kingdom with each book carefully cataloged, each customer treated like a puzzle she was determined to solve. She was precise, efficient, and intimidating in a way that reminded me of the headmistress at my old school.

But there was warmth beneath the rough edges.

"You organize like someone who finds peace in order," she remarked one afternoon, watching me straighten a row of books for the third time.

I didn't know what to say to that.

I had been holding my breath for months, waiting for someone to look at me and see through the cracks. But Mrs. Parker never asked where I came from or why I flinched at sudden noises. She just handed me a cup of chai and told me to stop working through my lunch breaks.

The bookstore became my world. I learned the rhythms of the regulars like the professor who always bought obscure poetry collections, the teenager who spent hours reading fantasy novels in the corner, the woman who only ever asked for recommendations on rainy days.

I found comfort in the weight of books, in the quiet shuffle of pages turning.

For the first time in years, I felt invisible in a way that was safe.

Linda never stopped pushing. She was relentless in her efforts to remind me that life existed outside the tiny cocoon I had built for myself.

"You can't just work and sleep forever," she declared one evening, waving a paintbrush at me like a weapon. "That's not living, Izzy."

"I like my life," I countered, curled up in the armchair in her studio.

She snorted. "No, you like avoiding it."

She wasn't wrong.

Linda pulled me into her world of art shows in hidden

galleries, late-night walks along the river, impromptu road trips just to chase the sunrise.

She forced me to remember that joy existed, even if I didn't always feel like I deserved it.

"You're not her anymore," she told me once, watching as I traced circles in my coffee cup. "You don't have to carry her ghost with you everywhere you go."

I wanted to believe her but the past still lingered. No matter how much I tried to bury it, the past had a way of slipping through the cracks.

Some nights, I still woke up gasping, heart pounding, theechoes of water lapping against the shore, of voices whispering my name in the dark.

I still hesitated before giving my name to strangers, still avoided cameras, still scanned newspaper headlines just to be sure.

I had a routine for moments of panic, to breathe in, breathe out, remind myself I was here, now, in a life that belonged to me.

Most days, it worked.

Most days, I felt almost whole.

Then there was Daniel. He started showing up at the bookstore more often.

At first, it was casual. A book here, a conversation there. Always easy, always with that same warm curiosity in his eyes.

Then it became something more.

He lingered longer. Brought coffee. Asked about my favorite books, my favorite places. He didn't pry, didn't press. He just listened.

And I found myself wanting to talk to him.

It terrified me.

The way he really saw me. Not as someone to be pitied or saved, but simply as a person.

One evening, as I was locking up the store, I found him waiting outside.

"Walk with me?" he asked.

I hesitated. I should have said no. I should have gone home and buried myself in the comfort of my solitude.

Instead, I nodded.

We walked through the quiet streets, the air thick with the scent of rain and earth.

"I feel like I should know more about you by now," he mused.

I forced a small smile. "Maybe I like being mysterious."

His gaze flickered with something unreadable. "Or maybe you're just hiding."

I stopped walking. My breath caught.

He didn't apologize for the words, didn't take them back. He just looked at me, waiting, like it was my choice how much of myself I was willing to give.

And for the first time in a long time, I wanted to give something. Just a small piece.

"I used to be someone else," I admitted softly.

Daniel didn't ask who. Didn't push. He just nodded.

"Well, whoever you were, I like who you are now."

I swallowed hard. For the first time in years, the weight of my past didn't feel quite so heavy. And as we walked through the quiet streets, I realized something terrifying. Maybe, just maybe, I was starting to belong.

21

PRESENT

I don't sleep much these days. Not since Noah disappeared.

At first, I told myself it was just adrenaline, that my body was too wired, too raw with panic to rest. But as the days stretched into weeks, exhaustion settled deep into my bones, and still, sleep refused to come. I close my eyes, and the inside of my head is nothing but questions.

Where is he?

Is he scared?

Is he safe?

Is it my fault?

I wake up sweating, sheets tangled around me, my breath shallow and sharp. Sometimes I dream about him. Sometimes I don't. And sometimes, I dream of nothing at all which is worse.

There's something off about the house.

It isn't just the emptiness, not just the silence where Noah's voice used to be, the toy cars that no longer clutter the floor, the quiet air so thick and stale it feels like the walls themselves are holding their breath. It's something else.

Something small.

Things aren't where I left them.

A glass I was drinking from disappears overnight. A book I left on the couch turns up on the shelf. The back door is unlocked in the morning, even though I know I locked it the night before.

I keep telling myself it's just my mind playing tricks on me. Stress does that to people.

But there's a feeling in my stomach that won't go away. A low, pulsing tension that makes my skin prickle every time I step into an empty room.

I don't like the house at night. It feels different. Like something is waiting. Like something is watching.

I wake to the sound of movement downstairs.

My body tenses, a sharp inhale catching in my throat. I sit up too quickly, heart racing. There's a dull moment of panic before I recognize the soft sound of footsteps, the unmistakable clink of a mug being set down on the counter.

Claire.

I push my hair back from my damp forehead. She must have let herself in. It's not the first time.

Since Noah disappeared, Claire has been **everywhere**. She checks in every day, showing up with coffee, bringing over food I forget to eat, sitting beside me in silence when I feel like I'm slipping into some kind of empty, hollow space.

I don't ask how she gets in.

She has a key. I gave it to her months ago, back when things were normal, when it seemed like a good idea to have someone I trusted be able to come and go.

I drag myself out of bed, wrapping a blanket around my shoulders as I make my way downstairs. The house is dim, bathed in the quiet glow of the kitchen light. Claire sits at the table, fingers curled around a steaming mug, absently flipping through the book I left out yesterday.

She looks up when she sees me, her face softening.

"Hey," she murmurs, like she's talking to a wounded animal. "I didn't mean to wake you."

I shake my head, pulling the blanket tighter. "Couldn't sleep anyway."

She studies me for a moment before nodding toward the chair across from her. "Sit. I made tea."

I don't argue. I slide into the chair, letting the warmth of the mug seep into my palms.

Claire watches me carefully, her gaze unreadable.

"You need to take care of yourself, Izzy."

I huff out a breath, shaking my head. "I don't even know what that looks like anymore."

She reaches out, brushing my wrist lightly. "Then let me do it for you."

Her words settle into the silence between us, lingering longer than they should.

I don't answer. I don't know how to.

Instead, I take a sip of my tea, the heat burning down my throat, grounding me.

Claire sighs, leaning back in her chair. "You're exhausted."

I nod.

"You haven't been yourself lately," she continues, and there's something gentle about the way she says it, something that makes my throat tighten.

I swallow hard. "I don't feel like myself."

Claire tilts her head, watching me. "You're stressed. You're overwhelmed. It makes sense that things feel... off."

I blink at her. "What do you mean?"

She hesitates. "You told me some things have been moving around the house. Things not being where you left them."

I nod slowly again.

Claire offers me a small, careful smile. "Maybe you're just

forgetting. Maybe you're sleepwalking, or just... moving things without realizing it."

I exhale, shaking my head. "I don't think—"

"Izzy." She cuts me off gently. "You're grieving."

My stomach clenches.

She leans forward, her voice soft. "Your brain is in survival mode right now. It's normal to feel like things are slipping. But you're not alone, okay? I'm here."

I stare down at my tea, focusing on the warmth against my fingers, trying to ignore the nagging feeling pressing against my ribs.

She's right. I know she's right.

I've read about trauma, about how the mind copes. I know people forget things, do things without realizing it like misplace objects and convince themselves they were taken.

That's what this is. Just my brain breaking apart at the seams.

Claire reaches out again, squeezing my hand.

"Let me help you, Izzy."

I look up at her, and she's watching me with such care, such genuine concern, that a sting of tears presses at the back of my throat.

I nod, just once.

Her smile is warm, reassuring. "Good," she murmurs. "Now drink your tea."

I do and for the first time in days, I let myself believe that maybe, just maybe, everything will be okay.

22

PAST

The first time I met Claire, I was just beginning to feel like myself again.

It had been nearly a year since I left my old life behind, nearly a year since I had whispered my new name to strangers, praying they wouldn't recognize the ghost of who I used to be.

By then, Richmond had become familiar, almost comfortable. The bookstore was steady, Linda was relentless, and Daniel had become an unexpected presence in my life. I was still careful, still cautious, but I was learning how to breathe again.

And then Claire arrived.

It was a rainy afternoon, the kind where the world felt like it had shrunk to the space beneath your umbrella.

I was in a coffee shop, a small place tucked between two brick buildings, its windows fogged up from the warmth inside. I had taken my usual corner table, my fingers curled around a cup of tea, my eyes unfocused as I pretended to read.

I wasn't really paying attention to anyone else. And then, someone sat down across from me.

"Sorry," she said quickly, pushing damp hair from her face.

"I think I just escaped a very awkward date, and I needed a landing spot. Mind if I hide here for a minute?"

I blinked at her, caught off guard.

She was about my age, maybe a little younger. She had sharp, clever eyes and a quick, apologetic smile. Something about her energy felt effortless, like she belonged anywhere she went.

Before I could decide whether to send her away, she huffed a sigh and set her phone down between us.

"Blind dates are the worst."

I hesitated. Then, cautiously, I said, "Bad?"

She rolled her eyes. "Bad is an understatement. He started talking about our future before we even ordered drinks. I don't even know his last name."

I surprised myself by laughing. It was a small sound, rusty from lack of use, but real.

She grinned. "Oh, thank God. You look like the kind of person who'd tell me if I was being overdramatic."

I glanced at the empty seat she had stolen. "You did just sit down with a complete stranger."

Her smile widened. "Technically, you could've told me to leave. That makes you an accomplice."

I shook my head, half amused, half wary. I had spent so much time avoiding people, keeping my world small and safe, that the ease of this moment caught me off guard.

She stuck out her hand. "Claire."

I hesitated for a fraction of a second before shaking it. "Izzy."

The name still felt foreign sometimes, but she accepted it without question.

And just like that, Claire became a part of my world.

At first, it was casual. A chance meeting turned into another. The next time I saw her, it was at the bookstore. She wandered through the shelves like she belonged there, pausing now and then to run her fingers over the spines.

"You again," she said, grinning when she spotted me behind the counter.

"You found my hiding place," I said dryly.

She shrugged. "It's a small city. Or maybe we have the same taste in books and coffee."

I wanted to keep my distance. I had worked too hard to rebuild my life, to keep my past buried. Letting someone new in meant more questions, more risks.

But Claire didn't push. She didn't pry. She was just there. And before I realized what was happening, she had slipped into my life like she had always been meant to be there.

Claire was easy to be around. She had an effortless warmth, the kind that made you feel like you'd known her for years instead of weeks.

She made me laugh. She teased without cruelty, listened without expectation. And for the first time in a long time, I found myself relaxing around someone new.

It wasn't just that she was kind. It was that she understood something unspoken.

She never asked me about my past. Never made me feel like I had to explain the gaps in my story.

Some people probe without realizing they're doing it. They ask where you grew up, what your family is like, if you've always lived here.

Claire didn't. She let silence exist without trying to fill it. It was a relief I hadn't known I needed.

The first time I let her into my home, it was raining again. She had shown up at the bookstore drenched, her umbrella useless against the wind.

"You're freezing," I said, pulling her inside before I could second-guess myself.

She kicked off her shoes, laughing as she wrung out her hair. "I think the universe is testing me."

I made tea while she curled up on my couch, looking around my small apartment with quiet curiosity.

"This place suits you," she said after a moment.

I glanced around. It was still mostly bare, just bookshelves, a few paintings Linda had forced on me, and a secondhand chair by the window.

"It's temporary," I said automatically.

Claire tilted her head, watching me. "Is it?"

I didn't answer.

Over time, she became part of my routine. We met for coffee, wandered through bookstores, spent long afternoons talking about nothing. She was the kind of person who made the world feel less lonely. And I needed that.

I didn't know how much until one evening, when I caught myself reaching for my phone just to tell her something funny that had happened at work.

The realization made my stomach twist. Letting people in had never ended well for me. But Claire felt different. Safe. And for the first time in years, I let myself believe that maybe, just maybe, I could have a friend again.

Claire slipped into my life so effortlessly, I almost didn't realize how much space she had claimed. She was there in the small moments, the quick text messages, the coffee shop encounters, the casual "I was in the neighborhood" drop-ins. It felt natural, easy, like she had been a part of my world all along.

I had spent so much time keeping people at arm's length that I had forgotten what it was like to have a real friend.

Claire filled the gaps before I even noticed they were empty.

One afternoon at the bookstore, I had a run-in with a customer that left my hands shaking.

It wasn't anything dramatic—just a man who lingered too long, his gaze a little too focused, his questions a little too pointed.

"Where are you from?"

"Do you live alone?"

"Do you have family in town?"

I had answered carefully, each response measured, neutral. But by the time he left, I felt that old, familiar fear creeping up my spine.

Claire found me ten minutes later, standing behind the counter, gripping the edge of the register like it was the only thing keeping me upright.

"Hey," she said softly, brows furrowed in concern. "What's wrong?"

I tried to brush it off. "Nothing. Just a weird customer."

She didn't accept that. She never did.

"Tell me."

So, I did.

I expected her to tell me I was overreacting. That I had imagined the tension. That I was being too careful, too paranoid.

Instead, she nodded, her expression unreadable.

"I don't like that," she murmured. "Do you want me to stay for a bit?"

I hesitated, then exhaled. "No, I'm okay."

But something about the way she asked so simply, without hesitation, unraveled something in me.

She wasn't just being polite. She wasn't just offering because she thought she had to. She meant it.

I realized then how much I had missed that. The quiet

presence of someone who would stand beside you, no questions asked.

She made Richmond feel like home. Before Claire, Richmond had always felt like a temporary stop. A place I was borrowing until I found somewhere better, somewhere safer.

But she anchored me in ways I hadn't expected.

She found places that became ours. A late-night diner with the best pancakes, a used bookstore that always smelled like lavender and dust, a hidden park with a pond where we sat for hours talking about nothing.

I caught myself thinking, Maybe I don't have to leave.

The thought terrified me. Because if I stayed, it meant I was building something real. It meant I had something to lose. And I wasn't sure I was ready for that.

She understood my walls without questioning them. Claire never asked me too many personal questions. She didn't push about my past.

When I hesitated before answering something, she let the silence settle instead of filling it with curiosity.

Most people don't know how to do that. It was why I had let my guard down around her so easily. She never made me feel like I had to explain myself and after years of being defined by my mistakes, by the whispers and accusations, that felt like freedom.

One night, long after I had closed the bookstore, my phone buzzed with a text.

Claire: Outside.

I frowned, glancing at the time. It was nearly midnight.

When I pulled the curtain back, I saw her standing on the sidewalk, arms crossed, wearing an oversized sweater like she had just rolled out of bed.

I opened the door. "What are you doing here?"

She grinned, unbothered by the late hour. "Thought you might want company."

I hesitated. "Did I say I did?"

"No. But I know you, and I know you probably spent all night in your own head."

I exhaled, half amused, half exasperated. "You're impossible."

She shrugged. "That's why you like me."

She wasn't wrong.

I let her in.

We sat on the couch, drinking tea, talking about nothing important.

She never asked why I had been quiet that day. She never asked why I had trouble sleeping. She just knew. And for the first time in years, I let someone else carry the silence with me.

Claire and Daniel met by accident.

It was a Sunday morning, and we were at our usual coffee shop, huddled over a shared plate of croissants when I saw him walk in.

I hadn't expected to see him there.

His eyes flicked across the café, landing on me almost immediately.

I felt my pulse skip, that familiar, quiet pull between us. Claire noticed.

I saw the way her gaze darted between us, the way her lips curled slightly, as if she had just discovered something amusing.

He walked over.

"Morning," he said, voice warm, easy.

"Morning," I echoed.

Claire arched a brow, clearly enjoying herself. "Are you going to introduce us?"

I sighed. "Claire, this is Daniel. Daniel, Claire."

She stuck out her hand, all confidence and charm. "Nice to finally meet you. I've heard a lot about you."

I shot her a look. "No, you haven't."

Daniel smirked. "Now I'm curious."

Claire just shrugged, eyes sparkling. "I'm just saying, I knew there was someone keeping you distracted."

I groaned. "You're the worst."

She grinned. "I know."

She made it impossible not to let her in. Claire became my constant. The friend who texted me random thoughts at odd hours. The person who showed up at my door when she sensed something was wrong. The one who made me feel like maybe, just maybe, I wasn't alone anymore.

She was warm, steady, safe.

For the first time in years, I had someone who felt like home. Because when you've spent so long drowning, you welcome the hand that pulls you to shore.

Present

The wind howls outside, threading through the trees like a ghost, rattling the old wooden shutters against the glass. But inside, everything is still. Warm. Safe. I watch him sleep.

His small chest rises and falls in slow, steady breaths, golden curls fanned out across the pillow. The quilt is pulled up to his chin, tiny fingers curled around the fabric like it's the only thing anchoring him.

He is so perfect. So mine.

I brush a hand over his forehead, pushing his hair back, reveling in the softness. He doesn't stir this time. He's exhausted. That's good. Sleep will help. Sleep will make him forget.

I have waited so long for this moment.

Years of planning, patience, and watching her, watching them, have led to this. Every detail had to be just right. The waiting, the notes, the fear. I had to make her weak. I had to break her.

Because only then could I take what was always meant to be mine.

Noah.

I reach out and run my fingers through his curls again. He whimpers softly in his sleep, shifting under the covers.

His room is just as I imagined it would be. Just as I prepared it to be.

The old wooden bed, painted the kind of white you don't see anymore. The delicate quilt, stitched with tiny stars. The bookshelf filled with real books, hardcovers, worn with love, stories that matter. None of that plastic, mass-produced nonsense other children are given.

A rocking horse stands in the corner, its wood polished to a soft shine. A small chest at the foot of the bed holds the toys I chose for him. Not flashy, mind-numbing distractions, but simple things. A stuffed rabbit with long, floppy ears. A set of wooden building blocks, hand-painted with letters and numbers. A puzzle, already laid out on the old rug, waiting for him to finish.

Everything is perfect. Just as I always planned. Just as we always should have had.

He stirs. A small whimper. His breath quickens. Then his lashes flutter open.

His little face scrunches in confusion, and for a moment, he just blinks at me. Then his small body stiffens, his hands tightening into fists.

His voice is small, barely above a whisper. "Where's Mommy?"

I smile, soft and reassuring.

"Don't worry, Little One," I murmur, smoothing his curls again. "You're safe now. I'll take care of you."

His tiny brow furrows, lips pressing together.

The way he doesn't understand yet hurts. The way he still thinks he belongs to her.

"I want my Mommy." His voice is more certain now, a quiet demand.

I sigh, shaking my head.

Poor thing. Poor, confused thing.

"Shh, sweetheart," I whisper, cupping his small cheek. "She doesn't love you the way I do."

He flinches, pulling back, his little fingers digging into the quilt. "Yes, she does."

The words stab into my chest, but I smile anyway. Because I knew this would take time.

"You don't have to worry anymore," I tell him gently. "She let you go. I saved you."

Tears well in his big, brown eyes. "No."

His breath comes faster now, his small chest rising and falling in shallow gasps. He looks around the room, taking in the old-fashioned furniture, the wooden beams of the ceiling, the heavy curtains drawn over the windows.

He doesn't recognize anything.

Good.

This is not her world. This is ours.

"I want to go home," he whispers and I feel my smile falterjust slightly.

I sit up straighter, smoothing the front of my dress, forcing my voice to remain steady. "This is home now."

He shakes his head, curls bouncing. "I want Daddy."

The words snap something inside me.

For a moment, just a moment, I grip the blanket too tightly.

He sees it and his breath catches. He is heavy-headed from the sleeping pills I crushed into his milk.

I force myself to exhale, to smile."You don't need them anymore, sweetheart," I say softly.

I reach for the cup of warm milk on the nightstand and press it gently into his small hands.

His fingers tremble as he takes it, looking up at me, uncertain.

My smile deepens.

"You're mine now, Little One."

Outside, the wind howls louder, whistling through the trees, rattling the walls of our house.

The world is far away.

No one will find us here.

And Noah...

Noah will love me.

He hesitates, the warm cup of milk shaking slightly in his small hands. His big, brown eyes flick up to me, uncertain, his bottom lip trembling.

I watch him carefully, my expression soft, patient.

He's afraid. *That's natural.*

All children fear change. They cling to what they know, even when what they know is wrong. Even when it's hurting them.

But he will see. He will understand.

I lean in slightly, tucking a stray curl behind his ear. "Drink, sweetheart," I murmur. "It'll help you feel better."

He sniffs, his little fingers tightening around the ceramic cup. He doesn't move to sip it, but he doesn't push it away either.

That's progress.

I sit back, folding my hands neatly in my lap, watching as he glances around the room again, his eyes flicking over every detail—the bookshelf, the rocking horse, the thick, dark curtains. He shifts under the weight of the heavy quilt, his small body tense.

"I know this isn't what you're used to," I say gently. "But that's okay. You'll settle in soon."

His brow furrows. He's trying to be brave. Trying to make sense of something that doesn't fit in his world. He's still searching for logic. For the things his mother told him.

I exhale slowly, giving him space to think.

Children process grief in different ways. Some cry. Some lash out. Some retreat inward, curling into themselves like little turtles, waiting for the world to fix itself.

Noah is doing all three at once.

It breaks my heart.

But I will fix him. I will show him that I am not the enemy.

He shifts slightly, pulling the quilt up to his chin, his small voice barely above a whisper. "Did Mommy say I could stay here?"

My smile doesn't falter, but my fingers press together just a little tighter.

He's so innocent. So brainwashed.

I tilt my head slightly. "Your mother..." I pause, choosing my words carefully. "She doesn't always know what's best for you."

His tiny face scrunches, confusion deepening.

I sigh, reaching out to stroke his hair again. He flinches just slightly but I ignore it. He's testing boundaries. That's normal.

"She loves you," I continue, my voice as soft as silk. "But not the way I do."

He pulls back further under the quilt, his small fingers gripping the edge. "Mommy loves me lots."

A sharp, electric flash of something bitter rolls through me, but I shove it down, swallowing past it.

"She thinks she does." I let out a small, sad sigh. "But love isn't just about saying the words, Little One."

I brush my thumb against his cheek, gentle and warm.

"Love is about keeping you safe. And she," I shake my head, "she doesn't always make the right choices."

Noah's eyes shimmer with tears, and for the first time, a flicker of doubt dances across his little face.

I knew it. I knew the cracks would start to show.

"She let you go," I whisper, pressing my palm to my chest. "But I saved you."

His breath stutters, his tiny fingers curling into fists against the blanket. His bottom lip wobbles.

"I want to go home."

I inhale slowly, pushing down the frustration, replacing it with patience.

He doesn't understand yet. But he will. This isn't just a new home for him. This is a better home. A home where he won't be ignored. Where he won't be left behind while his mother drowns in her own mind, in her own past. Where he will finally be loved the way he deserves.

I press a soft kiss to his forehead, my fingers brushing gently against his temple.

"You are home, Little One."

Noah stiffens under my touch. His little heart is racing and I can feel it against my palm. But I don't pull away. Not yet. Because one day soon, he will realize the truth. One day soon, he will look up at me the way he once looked at her.

With trust.

With love. With the certainty that I am the only person in this world who will never let him go. And on that day, he will finally call me Mommy. And I will finally be whole again.

23

PAST

The apartment smelled of dust and stale air, like something long abandoned. Carrie stepped inside, pausing to let the silence settle over her like a heavy coat. The door clicked shut behind her, the lock sliding into place with a finality that made her exhale.

She had imagined this moment for years, returning to this space, this version of herself. The walls were the same dull off-white, the floor still creaked in all the places she remembered, and the kitchen light flickered when switched on, just as it always had.

Setting her bag down near the couch, she ran her fingers along the dust-coated surfaces, the gritty sensation grounding her. She breathed in deeply the scent of old wood, faint mildew, something metallic, something that had never quite faded.

She was home.

Moving slowly through the apartment, Carrie reacquainted herself with the space. The furniture remained just as she had left it, only now covered in a fine layer of dust. She trailed her fingertips along the back of the worn-out couch, memories of sleepless nights curled against its armrest washing over her.

She let out a slow breath. The air here felt different, thicker, like the walls still remembered what had happened between them.

She moved toward the desk in the corner, her fingers brushing over an old coffee ring on the surface, a relic from before. Before the hospital. Before the verdict. Before everything had been taken from her.

With slow, deliberate movements, she lowered herself into the desk chair and opened the laptop. The screen flickered to life, casting an eerie glow across her face. The old familiarity of it, the comfort of seeking, of knowing, settled into her bones.

She had spent years in the dark, waiting. Watching.

Now, it was time to step back into the world.

She opened the browser and typed in the name that had haunted her, taunted her, for four long years.

Isabel Carter.

The results flooded in instantly. Headlines. Images. Speculation.

The Lockwood Case: Four Years Later.

Where Is Isabel Carter Now?

A Life After Scandal.

Carrie's eyes scanned the words, her pulse steady, her breathing slow.

She had moved on. How dare she.

A new job. A new city. A new life. A second chance.

She clicked on an article, her eyes darting over the lines, absorbing the words. Isabel Carter had rebuilt herself.

She had started fresh, wiping away the stains of the past as if they had never existed. No longer a nanny. No longer the woman caught in the scandal. No longer the one who had let two children slip through her fingers.

Now, she had a different life.

Carrie exhaled, slow and deep, the room tightening around

her. The faint throb of the refrigerator. The distant wail of a siren from the street below. The muted glow of the screen reflecting in her eyes.

She let her head fall back against the couch, her lips barely parting as she whispered,

"She doesn't deserve another chance."

A slow, curling smile crept across her lips. The world had forgiven Isabel Carter.

Carrie never would.

She reached for the drawer beside the desk, pulling it open with a quiet scrape. Beneath a layer of old papers and forgotten trinkets lay a small, battered notebook.

She lifted it carefully, brushing off the dust.

Inside, pages and pages of notes, sketches, and timelines filled the space. Newspaper clippings, some yellowed with age, were taped meticulously to the pages.

She flipped through them slowly, tracing old ink with her fingertips.

Articles about the verdict. About the media frenzy. About the aftermath. About Isabel Carter slipping away, disappearing into a new existence. Carrie had waited. And waited. Now, she would remind the world that some ghosts do not stay buried.

Her fingers tightened around the notebook. She had work to do.

The night outside was still, the city holding its breath. Carrie leaned against the window, watching the world move on without her.

Lights flickered in distant buildings. Strangers living lives untouched by the things she carried. She imagined Isabel somewhere out there, tucked into a quiet house, comfortable, safe.

Carrie smiled. She turned from the window, walked back to the desk, and opened her laptop once more.

Her fingers hovered over the keys. It was time to send a message.

24

PRESENT

The screen glows in the dimly lit room, my fingers moving restlessly over the trackpad, clicking, scrolling, searching. The cursor blinks, waiting, urging me forward.

My eyes burn from hours of reading old articles, faded photographs, snippets of gossip columns dissecting the Lockwood tragedy like vultures picking at a carcass.

The same headlines. The same accusations.

"Neglectful Nanny to Blame for Tragic Drowning of Lockwood Twins."

"Careless or Criminal? The Unanswered Questions in the Lockwood Case."

"Evelyn Lockwood's Public Outcry: 'My Children Were Left to Die.'"

I clench my jaw, swallowing against the sickening wave of nausea rising in my throat. I don't need to read it again. I lived it.

Instead, I dig deeper, past the mainstream coverage, past the courtroom photos and press releases.

I search for Evelyn. Because it has to be her.

Noah is gone, and Evelyn has every reason to want me to suffer.

I scan through articles on the Lockwoods, interviews, financial reports, the slow unraveling of Oliver and Evelyn's marriage after the twins died. Their downfall was public, messy, played out in the pages of every major paper. Accusations of an affair with a woman called Carrie.

Oliver moved his business dealings overseas before eventually fading from the public eye. Evelyn became a recluse.

Then, an old business article catches my eye.

"Oliver Lockwood: The Man Behind Lockwood Capital's International Expansion."

It's a stiff, corporate feature, full of stock phrases and over-polished PR language. But it's the accompanying photograph that steals my breath.

Oliver sits at his desk, grinning smugly at the camera, his suit crisp, his posture relaxed. Beside him stands a business associate, someone whose name I don't recognize, whose presence I don't care about.

Because in the background, near the bookshelf, slightly out of focus but unmistakable is her.

My blood turns to ice.

She's younger in the photo, her hair slightly longer, her face softer, but it's her. The same sharp cheekbones. The same eyes.

The woman I know as Claire. Only this article calls her Carrie.

I push back from the desk, my pulse hammering in my ears.

No.

No.

I shake my head, scrambling and clicking on the image, enlarging it, bringing her face into sharper focus.

It doesn't make sense. It can't make sense.

But it does.

Claire—Carrie—was in Oliver Lockwood's office.

She knew him. More than knew him.

I suck in a sharp breath, trying to steady myself, but the

ground beneath me feels unsteady like the entire world has tilted off its axis.

I click away from the article and open a new search.

"Carrie Oliver Lockwood."

"Carrie Oliver Lockwood affair."

I dig and dig until I find it.

A court record.

A sealed case.

Oliver Lockwood. Carrie—her last name. It was something else back then, something common, something forgettable.

And a mention of paternity rights.

Oh my God.

My throat tightens as I click on another result.

A gossip blog from years ago. A barely noticeable mention of Oliver's mistress. A woman he got pregnant.

I slap a hand over my mouth.

Carrie was pregnant with Oliver's child.

I sit frozen for what feels like hours. I think about the things I have said to Claire. About Oliver. About the twins. About Evelyn.

Forcing my fingers to move, I pull up every possible contact listing for Evelyn Lockwood, my breath coming in short, sharp bursts.

I find a number. It's old and listed under one of her last known business ventures before she disappeared from society.

I hit call.

It rings. And rings.

Then a voice, sharp and familiar, crackles through the receiver.

"Who is this?"

I grip the phone tighter. "Evelyn." My voice is unsteady, but I force strength into it. "It's Isabel Warren."

Silence. A sharp inhale. Then, a quiet, disdainful chuckle. "Well. I can't say I expected to hear from you."

I close my eyes, inhaling deeply. "Evelyn, I need to ask you something. It's important."

She scoffs. "And what makes you think I care?"

I don't have time for this. I don't have time for her games.

I grit my teeth. "It's about *Carrie."*

A pause. Then her voice shifts to be sharper now, but tinged with something else. Recognition.

"What about her?"

I swallow hard. "She knew Oliver, didn't she?"

Evelyn lets out a dry, humorless laugh. "Knew him? Oh, darling, she loved him."

My stomach churns.

"She was his little pet," Evelyn continues, her tone dripping with disdain. "His distraction. One of many."

I press a hand to my forehead, my skin clammy. "She was pregnant, wasn't she?"

Silence. Then, "Yes," Evelyn says simply.

I squeeze my eyes shut.

No, no, no.

"She lost the baby," Evelyn continues, her voice void of sympathy. "Some kind of complication, I don't remember. Didn't care, really. I was too busy dealing with my own life falling apart because of that man."

I shake my head, gripping the phone tighter. "So that's it? She lost the baby, and Oliver—what? He left her?"

Evelyn scoffs. "Of course he did. He never kept them, darling."

Bile rises in my throat.

Carrie—Claire—lost a child. Oliver abandoned her. And now she's taken mine.

I don't even realize I've stopped breathing until Evelyn's voice cuts through the static in my head.

"What is this about, Isabel?" She pauses. "Why are you calling me?"

My hands are shaking. My entire body feels numb.

I suck in a sharp breath. "She' taken my son."

A beat of silence. Then Evelyn laughs. A cold, cruel, delighted sound.

"Oh, Isabel," she murmurs, her voice dripping with venom. "Maybe now you finally understand."

My stomach drops.

"What?" My voice is barely above a whisper.

Evelyn exhales, amused. "What it feels like to have something you love taken from you."

Her words slam into me, knocking the air from my lungs.

Tears sting my eyes.

She doesn't care. She wants me to suffer.

"Go to hell," I whisper, my voice shaking.

Evelyn chuckles again. "Already there, darling. You'll be joining me soon."

And then the line goes dead.

I stare at the phone, my entire body trembling.

The truth is here, sitting right in front of me. Claire is Carrie. Carrie loved Oliver. Carrie lost his child.

And now, she wants mine.

She's dangerous. Deranged.

My chair scrapes against the floor as I shove away from the desk, my pulse hammering in my ears.

The house feels too small, too tight, closing in around me.

My breath is shallow, my thoughts a tangled mess, but one thing is clear. I need to tell Dan. Now.

I race down the stairs, my bare feet slapping against the hardwood.

Dan is sitting on the couch, hunched forward, elbows resting on his knees. He barely looks up as I burst into the room.

"Dan." My voice is raw, frantic. "Claire isn't who she says she is."

His head snaps up, his tired, bloodshot eyes narrowing. "What?"

I shake my head violently, gripping the back of the couch for support, my body still trembling.

"Claire, she's not Claire." The words tumble from me, wild and unhinged. "She's Carrie."

Dan blinks, his exhaustion momentarily overridden by sheer confusion.

"Izzy, what the hell are you talking about?"

"I found a picture." My voice is sharp, urgent. "An old one. Of Oliver Lockwood in his office. She's there, Dan. Standing right in the background."

I swallow hard, forcing myself to slow down.

"She knew him. She was involved with him. She was pregnant with his child."

Dan straightens, his posture shifting, the doubt in his expression flickering with something else, something darker.

"She lost the baby," I continue, my voice hoarse. "And now, Dan, don't you see? She took Noah."

Dan exhales sharply, running both hands down his face, shaking his head. "Jesus Christ."

He's trying to process it. Trying to make it fit. I don't let him stop.

"I called Evelyn," I add, my voice trembling. "She confirmed it. Carrie had an affair with Oliver. She lost the baby. And then she just... disappeared."

My stomach twists.

"And now she's here. In our lives. She's been right next to us this whole time."

Dan pushes off the couch, pacing across the room, rubbing his jaw, his breathing shallow.

"We need to call Birch."

I nod frantically. "Yes."

Dan doesn't hesitate. He grabs his phone, scrolling quickly before pressing call. He paces as it rings, his fingers tapping against his thigh.

"Detective Birch," he says as soon as the line connects. "We need you to come to the house. Now."

A pause. I can't hear Birch's response, but Dan's next words are clipped, tense.

"It's about Noah. And Claire." His jaw tightens. "She's not who we thought she was."

Another pause. Then Dan nods. "Alright." He hangs up, exhaling sharply. "He's on his way."

I sink onto the couch, my legs shaking.

Dan sits beside me, running a hand over his face. "If she took him..." His voice cracks slightly, his hands clenching into fists. "Why hasn't she contacted us? Why hasn't she asked for something?"

I shake my head. "She doesn't want a ransom, Dan. She doesn't want revenge."

My stomach clenches as the words form, as the realization settles deep into my bones.

"She wants a child."

Dan looks at me then, his face drained of color, his breath shaky. And I know *he believes me now.*

Birch arrives within the hour, stepping into the house with the same cool, detached demeanor as always.

"Alright," he says, glancing between me and Dan as he pulls out his notepad. "Tell me what you've got."

I shove the laptop toward him, my hands still unsteady. "Look."

He leans down, scanning the image on the screen. The photo of Oliver in his office. The blurred figure in the background.

"She was there," I say, my voice urgent. "She knew him. She was part of his life."

Birch frowns slightly, clicking through the other documents I pulled up—old articles, court records, Evelyn's statements.

Then he exhales through his nose, straightening up. "So, Claire's real name is Carrie. And she had an affair with Oliver Lockwood."

I nod. "Yes."

"She lost the baby," Birch continues, tapping the side of the laptop. "And now you think she took Noah."

"Yes." My breath stutters. "She inserted herself into my life, Birch. She got close to me, to my family. To Noah."

I shake my head. "She's been planning this for years."

Birch rubs his jaw, his expression unreadable. "I'll look into her."

My chest tightens. "That's *not* enough."

Birch's gaze flicks to me, sharp. "Pretending to be someone else isn't a crime, Mrs. Warren."

I stare at him, my pulse pounding. "She *kidnapped my son.*"

"We don't have evidence of that," Birch says smoothly. "Not yet."

My stomach turns.

Dan steps forward, his voice tight with frustration. "She's *missing*, Birch. She disappeared just after Noah did. That's not a coincidence."

Birch exhales through his nose, flipping his notepad closed. "I'll start running checks. See what I can dig up."

Dan's jaw clenches. "That's it?"

Birch looks at me then, his expression unreadable. "I need more than suspicion to get a warrant, Mrs. Warren."

Anger coils in my chest, hot and suffocating. "And how long will that take? While she has *my son*?"

He doesn't answer. Because we all know the truth.

No one is moving fast enough. And every second that passes is another second Noah is getting *further away*.

I dig my nails into my palms, forcing myself to breathe, forcing myself to think.

If the police won't act, I will. I don't care what it takes. I will find him. And I will bring him home.

25

PRESENT

Evelyn Lockwood sat alone in the grand, echoing silence of her estate. The Lockwood house had always felt too vast, even when it had been full, when the halls had echoed with laughter, when small feet had pattered across polished wood, when Charlotte's tiny voice had called for her mother, a familiar note in the melody of life.

Now, the house felt like a mausoleum.

She traced the edge of a picture frame with her fingertips, the glass cool beneath her touch. Inside it, Theo and Charlotte grinned back at her, frozen in time. Theo had been five in this photo, his dark curls unruly, his eyes sparkling with mischief. Charlotte, barely three, had clutched his sleeve as she always did, looking up at him with unwavering trust.

Evelyn inhaled sharply, closing her eyes against the flood of memories.

It had been seven years since the lake had swallowed them. Seven years since she had stood before the world, a mother laid bare by grief, demanding justice for the children who'd never had a chance to grow up.

Seven years since her name had filled every headline, since

the press had dissected every moment of her mourning, since the whispers had begun.

She had thought she had learned to live with it.

But grief was a living thing—it changed shape, but never truly left.

And now, it had returned.

The knock at the door startled her.

Evelyn wasn't expecting anyone. Few people visited anymore. Over the years, most of their old friends had drifted away, unable to bridge the widening chasm that loss had carved into the Lockwood family.

She set the frame aside and rose, smoothing her blouse as she walked to the door.

When she opened the door, she found a young woman standing there, rain still clinging to the shoulders of her trench coat, a notepad clutched tightly in one hand.

A journalist.

Evelyn knew the type. She had spent years dodging them, refusing to become another spectacle for the world to consume.

The woman—Lucy Collins, according to the name scrawled on her press badge—offered a hesitant smile.

"Mrs. Lockwood, I'm sorry to bother you."

Evelyn kept her face impassive. "I don't do interviews."

"I understand," Lucy said quickly. "This isn't about the past. It's about something happening now."

Something in her tone made Evelyn pause.

Lucy hesitated, then lowered her voice, as if the words themselves carried weight.

"There's a missing child. A boy."

Evelyn stiffened. She looked at the young woman standing there, rain still clinging to the shoulders of her trench coat, a notepad clutched tightly in one hand.

"The circumstances," Lucy continued carefully, "are... eerily similar."

A sick sense of dread curled in Evelyn's stomach. "Similar?"

"The mother—" Lucy faltered, watching Evelyn's reaction. "She's been accused of negligence. There are gaps in her story. Some people think she might be involved."

Evelyn's pulse thrummed in her ears. She had heard these words before. She had lived them.

"The mother's name," she said, already knowing the answer.

Lucy exhaled. "Isabel."

The sound of it was a knife.

For years, Evelyn had forced herself not to say it. Not to let it take up space in her mind, not to let herself wonder where the woman who had failed her children had gone.

She had tried to move on.

But now, Isabel was back in the headlines.

Evelyn stared at Lucy, her grip tightening on the doorframe.

"Why are you here?" she asked, her voice sharp.

Lucy shifted uncomfortably. "I think there's more to the story than what's being reported. I think Isabel Warren is hiding something. And I was hoping—"

"You were hoping I'd help you destroy her," Evelyn finished coldly.

Lucy blinked. "I—"

"You want to write about my grief?" Evelyn pressed. "Turn my children into a convenient tragedy to fuel some new scandal?"

Lucy's face flushed. "No, I—"

Evelyn's expression remained impassive.

"I don't have anything to say about Isabel," she said, her voice steady. "Not to you. Not to anyone."

She stepped back, gripping the edge of the door.

"Mrs. Lockwood, please—"

The door slammed shut.

Evelyn stood still, her breath coming in shallow gasps. She pressed a hand to her chest, as if trying to hold back the storm brewing inside her.

She had tried not to think about Isabel. But now, as the silence of the house closed in around her, she found herself reaching for the picture frame once more.

Theo and Charlotte. Frozen in time.

And Isabel, somewhere out there, accused again.

Evelyn didn't believe in fate. But maybe, just maybe, it was time to stop pretending she could outrun the past.

Evelyn Lockwood sat at the dining table, an untouched cup of tea growing cold beside her. Outside, the afternoon light cast long, fractured shadows across the marble floors. The house, always too quiet, felt even more cavernous now.

The weight of the journalist's visit clung to her like damp air. Isabel Warren. The name had once been a wound Evelyn had vowed never to reopen. And yet, here it was tearing through the walls she had spent years building.

She glanced at the empty seat across from her, the one where Oliver used to sit. It had been months since he left, but the absence still felt raw.

They hadn't divorced, not officially. Lockwoods didn't divorce. They simply unraveled in slow, painful increments, severing themselves from one another until they were nothing more than a name on paper.

Evelyn knew it had started long before he packed his bags.

The loss of Theo and Charlotte had hollowed their marriage even further, left it fragile, brittle. It was easy to pretend, for a time, that they could endure, that grief could be shared rather than suffered alone. But Oliver had retreated into his work, into more empty distractions Evelyn never asked about.

He had always been good at making himself scarce when things got difficult.

So, in the end, she let him go.

Now, she was alone with the ghosts. And Isabel Warren was back.

Evelyn's hands trembled as she reached for her phone.

She hesitated. Then, with slow precision, she opened a news article, her eyes scanning the headline.

MISSING CHILD CASE TAKES UNEXPECTED TURN—MOTHER UNDER SCRUTINY

The name struck her like a physical blow. Isabel Warren.

Or rather—Isabel Calloway.

Evelyn exhaled, her pulse quickening.

She had changed her name. She had started over. But even after all these years, trouble had found her again.

She clicked on the article.

The details were sparse. A three-year-old boy, gone without a trace. The mother's version of events uncertain, her past questionable. Evelyn could almost hear the same whispers, the same doubts that had followed Isabel seven years ago.

"She was the last one with them."

"She didn't see anything."

"How do children just... disappear?"

Evelyn wanted to close the article, to let it go, to pretend she wasn't here and wasn't doing this to herself. But she couldn't.

She scrolled further. There was a photo of Isabel, walking out of what appeared to be a police station, her face drawn, her hair unkempt, the same hollow look in her eyes that Evelyn remembered all too well.

The image stirred something dark within her. Seven years ago, she had looked just like that.

Evelyn had thought she buried that part of her life, the part consumed by tragedy, grief, and the endless, gnawing questions of what might have been different.

She had moved on. But fate, it seemed, wasn't finished with her.

She didn't even realize she had dialed his number until she heard the familiar voice on the other end.

"Evelyn?"

She closed her eyes. It had been months since they last spoke.

"Oliver," she said, her voice controlled. "Did you see the news?"

A pause. Then, carefully, "I did."

There was something measured about his tone, as though he had expected this call but wasn't sure what to do with it.

Evelyn exhaled slowly, gripping the phone tighter. "She's back."

"She never left," Oliver replied. "She just disappeared for a while."

Evelyn swallowed. She hated the way his voice still had the power to make her feel small, reminding her of the person she had been when they stood together, grieving, their children buried beneath the earth.

"Her son is missing," she said.

"I know."

"She's being questioned again."

"I know that too."

She hesitated. "Do you think she—"

"No."

His answer came quickly, without hesitation. It surprised her.

Evelyn had spent years convinced that Isabel had failed them in some irredeemable way, that even if she hadn't done something, she had let Theo and Charlotte slip through her fingers, let them vanish.

"Seven years is a long time," Oliver continued. "People change."

Evelyn let out a bitter laugh. "Do they?"

Oliver sighed, the kind of sigh that meant he didn't want to have this conversation.

"I just called to—" she began, but he cut her off.

"You called because you want to know if you should get involved."

Evelyn stilled.

"You don't have to," Oliver said quietly. "You don't owe her anything, Evelyn. This isn't your fight."

She wanted to agree. She wanted to let it go. But she thought of the way the reporter had looked at her, the way she had said, "The circumstances are eerily similar."

The past was knocking at her door again and she wasn't sure she had the strength to leave it unanswered.

Evelyn didn't sleep that night.

Instead, she went to the attic, where she had hidden everything away the photos, the newspaper clippings, the case files she had sworn she wouldn't keep but couldn't bring herself to throw away.

The box was exactly where she had left it, tucked behind old storage bins, untouched for years.

Her fingers hovered over the lid.

Then, slowly, she lifted it open.

Inside, the past waited.

Newspaper headlines, yellowed with time.

NANNY QUESTIONED IN MYSTERIOUS DROWNING OF LOCKWOOD CHILDREN.

NO CHARGES FILED IN LOCKWOOD TRAGEDY.

ISABEL WARREN—HOW DID SHE WALK AWAY?

There were photos too. Of Theo. Of Charlotte. And one of Isabel, walking past a sea of reporters, her face pale, her expression unreadable.

The weight of it settled over her, heavy, suffocating.

She reached for the article at the top of the pile: the last interview Isabel ever gave.

She read the words, her eyes scanning the familiar lines, the rehearsed statements. But something pulled her focus. Something she hadn't noticed before.

It was just a sentence. One small, insignificant sentence.

"I have nothing left to say. I just want to live my life."

And now, here she was again. Another missing child. Another investigation.

She had wanted to forget. She had wanted to move on. But the past wasn't done with her. And as she stared down at Isabel's name in black ink, she realized, neither was she.

26

PRESENT

The room is too small. The bed is too soft and the walls are all wrong. They aren't the blue ones with stars like at home. These are plain, boring white like the doctor's office. There's a window, but thick curtains keep it closed, and the air smells like flowers that aren't real.

I don't like it here.

I don't want to be here.

I want Mommy.

I sit on the bed, legs pulled up, arms wrapped around my stuffed bunny. He smells like home, like my real bed. Not this one. The sheets are scratchy, and the blanket smells like soap, but not the kind Mommy uses.

The door opens.

I jump a little. I try to be brave.

She comes in, smiling like a nice lady. But she isn't nice.

I don't know how I know, but I do.

She walks slowly, like she's trying not to scare me. But I'm already scared. I don't like how she watches me, how her smile is too big like when people on TV pretend to be happy.

She sits in the chair by the bed.

"Hi, sweetheart," she says. "How are you feeling?"

I don't say anything. My tummy hurts, but I don't tell her.

She tilts her head, eyes soft, waiting for me to answer. "I bet you're still a little sleepy, aren't you?"

I nod, because it's easier than not nodding.

Her smile grows wider.

"You've had a big day, haven't you?" She reaches out and brushes my hair back. I don't like it, but I don't move. I don't want to make her mad.

"Do you remember what I told you?" she asks, still soft, still nice.

I squeeze my bunny. I don't want to remember.

Her eyes flick to my hands, to the bunny.

"Oh, sweetheart," she says, "you don't have to be scared. I told you, didn't I?"

She leans in closer, so close I can smell her. She smells like flowers. Not Mommy flowers. Different ones.

"My name is Carrie," she says, like she's telling me a secret.

I don't say anything.

She reaches out again, smoothing my sleeve. "And I'm going to be your new mommy."

My heart starts pounding.

I shake my head before I can stop it. "No."

Her smile flickers, just for a second.

Then she laughs. "Oh, sweet boy, I know this is confusing." She tilts her head, like she's thinking really hard. "I know you miss her. But she's not coming back for you."

I squeeze my bunny tighter.

She watches me. Her smile is still there, but smaller now. Different. Scary.

"I know this is hard," she says, her voice softer, slower. "I know you're a little sad, but it's okay. Because I love you. And I'm going to take care of you."

My lip wobbles. I don't want to cry.

Mommy told me once that I was brave. I have to be brave.

Carrie keeps watching me, waiting for me to say something. When I don't, she nods, like she's made a decision.

"I know what will help," she says. She stands and walks to the dresser, the one with all the wrong clothes in it. She opens a drawer and pulls something out.

A book. It's not mine, but I know it.

She turns it over in her hands, fingers smoothing the cover. "Do you remember this one?"

I do.

Mommy used to read it to me. At bedtime, when the lights were low, and she would do the voices and make the silly faces.

My throat gets tight. I nod.

Carrie's smile comes back, big and warm like I should be happy. "I thought you would."

She comes back and sits on the bed this time, right next to me. I don't like it.

She opens the book, turns to the first page, and starts to read. Her voice is soft. Sweet. Almost like Mommy's. But it's not Mommy's.

As she reads, I feel tears in my eyes. I blink fast, so they don't fall.

She's pretending. Like a story. Like a game. Like a lie.

I don't say anything. I don't move.

I just sit there, trapped in the small, wrong room, listening to the pretend voice of the woman who says she's my new mommy.

But she isn't.

And I want to go home.

27

PRESENT

The station buzzes with low, monotonous activity, the kind that usually fades into the background. Phones ring, keyboards clack, officers converse in clipped, measured voices.

Detective Birch barely notices any of it.

His fingers hover over the keyboard, clicking through various databases, rerunning the search query for the fourth time, his gut twisting tighter with each failed result.

No records exist for a Claire Henderson.

Not in Virginia. Not in the surrounding states. Not anywhere.

The name is a phantom. A fabrication.

Birch exhales sharply through his nose, rubbing his jaw as a cold, creeping dread coils in his chest.

He leans back in his chair, rolling his shoulders before making a decision. He digs into the archives, his fingers flipping through old case files. Something about this feels wrong—familiar in a way he can't quite place, like an itch buried beneath his skin.

Then he sees it. Carrie Langley.

His stomach tightens. He carefully pulls the file out, laying it flat on his desk. The edges are worn, the paper slightly yellowed with time.

He flips it open and is immediately met with the photos.

A young woman barely out of her teens stares straight into the camera, her tangled hair framing her face like a curtain. But it's her eyes that catch him, unflinching, hollow, something too bright burning behind them.

A shiver creeps up his spine.

His fingers tighten around the file as he scans the documents inside.

Psychiatric evaluations. Arrest records. Detainment reports.

Each line is worse than the last.

"Displays obsessive tendencies. Delusional attachment to former employer, Oliver Lockwood."

"Erratic behavior following loss of pregnancy. Blames external forces for personal suffering."

"Fixation on recreating perceived 'lost family' scenario."

"Diagnosed with delusional disorder, with elements of erotomania and displaced maternal fixation."

Birch swallows hard, flipping through page after page of notes detailing her mental decline and the obsessive letters she sent Oliver even after he cut her off, the restraining orders Evelyn Lockwood filed against her.

Then, at the very bottom of the report, in sharp black ink:

Subject released from psychiatric care. Dated three years ago.

His stomach drops and a sinking, twisting, sick feeling washes over him. He slams the file shut and shoves his chair back from the desk so fast it scrapes against the floor. Grabbing his phone, he dials Detective Holloway's number, his fingers unsteady.

It rings once before the detective picks up.

"Holloway, listen to me. We have a serious problem."

Holloway doesn't need to ask questions.

The urgency in Birch's voice is enough to get him moving.

The moment the call ends, Birch is already grabbing his coat, heading toward the station archives. Holloway isn't the kind of guy to get spooked easily, and yet he'd sounded rattled. Birch isn't about to ignore that.

At his desk, he spreads the case file out in front of him, scanning every detail, every name, every thread that connects this woman to the past.

Carrie Langley.

Why hadn't he looked at her sooner?

Her name wasn't attached to any recent records. She had no criminal activity under Claire Henderson. But now, with this discovery, everything snaps into place.

Birch works methodically, piecing together what had been right in front of them the whole time.

First, Carrie's psychiatric history and her obsession with Oliver Lockwood, her erratic behavior after her pregnancy loss, the violent outbursts, the restraining orders Evelyn Lockwood filed against her.

Second, her disappearance after her release from psychiatric care, she vanished. No known address, no employment history, no financial records.

Then, three years later she reappears with a new name. A new life. And suddenly, she's right next to Isabel Warren.

Birch presses his lips into a tight line, his jaw clenching as he continues digging.

He pulls phone records.

There are traces of Claire—Carrie—popping up in different locations, but one thing stands out:

Frequent calls to a disposable number. Untraceable. Planned.

Birch exhales sharply, shaking his head. This woman is careful.

Then, he pulls up surveillance footage from local ATMs, security cameras—anywhere she might have appeared under her new identity.

One grainy image pops up.

Taken outside a gas station two weeks ago.

Claire—Carrie—is at the counter, buying supplies. Her face is partially turned away, but it's her. He knows it.

But it's not just the sight of her that makes his stomach drop.

It's what she's been buying.

Children's clothes.

Birch swallows the bile rising in his throat.

This wasn't impulsive, this was planned.

His fingers tighten around the edges of the file as everything clicks into place.

Carrie lost Oliver's child.

Carrie reinvents herself as Claire.

Carrie befriends Isabel—gets close to Noah.

And then, Carrie takes Noah.

He stands abruptly, shoving the file under his arm and heading straight for Holloway's office.

"Get a warrant," Birch snaps the moment he steps inside. "Now."

Holloway looks up, already nodding. "Way ahead of you."

Birch's jaw tightens. "We need to find her. Now."

Holloway picks up the phone and dials into dispatch, his voice clipped, controlled. He remembers the original case. He lived through it.

"This is Holloway. I need an immediate trace on Claire Henderson, real name Carrie Langley. Suspect in an ongoing kidnapping investigation."

Birch watches as the pieces begin to move, the station shifting into motion around them.

They have a name. They have a face. And now, finally, they have a trail.

28

PRESENT

The fire flickers low in the hearth, casting long shadows across the wooden floor. The house is silent, save for the crackling of burning logs and the occasional creak of old beams settling in the cold night air.

Outside, the wind howls through the trees, rattling the shutters. But inside, the room is warm, cocooned in golden firelight. Safe.

Our home.

Noah sits beside me on the old couch, his tiny body tucked against my side. He's still wary, but he isn't crying. That's progress. He clutches the stuffed rabbit I gave him, the one I picked out just for him, its fur soft from years of love.

He's wearing the pajamas I set out for him, striped blue cotton, just like the ones I imagined he would wear. They're a little big on him, but that's alright. He'll grow into them.

I smile, running my fingers through his hair, marveling at how soft his curls are and how perfect he is.

So much like the child I lost.

I press a gentle kiss to the top of his head. "You can call me Carrie now."

His little body stiffens slightly. He tilts his head up at me, confusion flickering in his deep brown eyes.

"Why?"

I stroke his cheek, my voice low, soothing. "Because that's my real name, sweetheart."

His brows knit together, his tiny hands tightening around the rabbit. "Mommy called you Claire."

I let out a quiet sigh, brushing his curls from his forehead. "She didn't know who I really was."

He hesitates, his small fingers twisting the fabric of his pajama top. "Mommy knows everything."

I keep my voice soft, patient. "Oh, my love. That's what she wanted you to think."

Noah stares at me, his little chest rising and falling in slow, uneven breaths.

I know what he's doing.

He's searching for the truth. Trying to make sense of something that doesn't fit in his small world.

I press my lips together, then sigh as if I'm reluctant to say the words. "Sweetheart, I know this is hard. But your mommy... she didn't always keep you safe."

His tiny hands tighten around the rabbit. "She does," he whispers. "She loves me."

I brush my fingers down his back, slow and steady. "She says she does," I murmur. "But love isn't just words, Little One. Love is about protecting you. And she didn't do that, did she?"

His small brow furrows. "Yes, she did."

I sigh again, stroking his arm, my voice laced with quiet sadness. "No, sweetheart. She let you go. And she let other children go, too."

He stiffens. "What?"

I tuck him closer, wrapping my arms around his small frame —warm, reassuring. "You don't know, do you?" I whisper against his hair. "She doesn't talk about them. Theo and Charlotte."

Noah swallows hard, his little fingers gripping my sleeve now. "Who?"

I sigh, rocking him gently, my voice hushed, like I'm telling him a bedtime story.

"Two little children, just like you. A boy and a girl. They were supposed to be safe, just like you were. But your mommy... she wasn't watching them. And they died."

Noah's breath hitches. His little body trembles.

I hold him tighter, stroking his back. "She was supposed to take care of them," I whisper. "And she failed."

Noah shakes his head against my shoulder. "No, no. Mommy loves me—"

"Oh, sweetheart," I murmur, kissing the top of his head. "She let them die. And now, she's let you go too."

He sniffles, his tiny hands pressing into my side, his whole body tense.

I hush him, rocking him gently, letting his small frame melt into mine.

"You don't have to be afraid anymore," I whisper, my lips brushing against his curls.

I squeeze my eyes shut, holding him so close I can feel his little heartbeat fluttering like a trapped bird against my chest.

"You're safe now, Little One."

I kiss his forehead, smoothing his curls back, pressing my cheek to the top of his head.

"You're mine now," I murmur. "You can call me Mommy if you like."

The fire crackles beside us, its warmth stretching across the room, wrapping us in its embrace.

Outside, the wind howls. But inside, we are exactly where we are meant to be.

Together.

29

PRESENT

The house feels colder than usual as I sit on the edge of the couch, phone clutched in my hand, my knee bouncing uncontrollably. The air is thick, heavy with something unspoken, the weight of dread pressing down on my chest.

The call comes just after midnight.

My phone vibrates violently on the coffee table, the sound shattering the silence. Dan is beside me, his head jerking up at the noise, his breath sharp and on the edge of sleep but never quite there.

I grab it before the second ring, my hands shaking.

"Holloway?" My voice is tight, breathless.

His voice is steady, controlled. "Izzy. Listen, I'm working with Birch now. We're looking for her." A pause. "But we don't have a location yet."

The words hit like a slap.

Not we found her. Not we know where Noah is. Just we don't have a location yet.

I shut my eyes, gripping the phone tighter.

Dan shifts beside me, sitting up straighter, his hand hovering over my knee like he wants to offer comfort but doesn't know how.

I push forward. "You have her real name. You know who she is. What the hell are you waiting for?"

"We're moving as fast as we can," Holloway says, his voice calm—almost too calm, like he's trying to keep me from unraveling.

It doesn't work.

I stand abruptly, pacing the length of the room, my heartbeat drumming against my ribs. "That's not fast enough. She's out there with my son, and you're telling me you don't even know where the hell she lives?"

Dan watches me carefully, his own face pale and strained, but he doesn't stop me.

Holloway exhales sharply. "Izzy, I get it—"

"No, you don't." My voice cracks. "You don't get it. You weren't there when she was in my house, sitting at my goddamn kitchen table, playing with my child." I let out a shaky breath. "She was right there, and I didn't see it. I didn't know."

I feel sick. I feel stupid.

Holloway sighs through the phone, the sound low and measured. "We're tracking any properties connected to her. We're going to find her, Izzy."

His voice is full of certainty. But I don't believe him. Not yet. Not fast enough.

I turn toward the window, staring out into the empty street. The police cars are still stationed outside, engines humming low in the cold night air. But they aren't moving. They aren't doing anything.

They're just waiting. And I don't trust them to act before it's too late.

I rub my forehead, my thoughts racing. Then I remember something. Holloway was there before, during the Lockwood investigation. Back when my face was plastered across every news station, every article dissecting what I had done.

Holloway wasn't the one leading the case, that was someone else, a man with small, cold eyes and a mouth always pressed into a tight, disapproving line. But Holloway had been there. He had stood in the background, had watched me sob through my statements, had listened as Evelyn Lockwood told the world I was a monster.

And when the press turned against me, when reporters camped outside my door, when people spat at me in the streets, Holloway had done nothing to stop it.

I stop pacing. "You worked my case before."

He hesitates. "Yes."

My stomach twists.

"You didn't believe me then," I whisper, the memory sharp, fresh, pressing against my ribs like a knife.

Another pause. "I wasn't the lead investigator on the Lockwood case, Izzy. But yes. I remember it."

I swallow hard. "And what did you think? Did you think I was guilty like everyone else?"

His silence is louder than anything he could have said.

I close my eyes, breathing through the weight of it. "And now?"

Now, when Noah is missing. When another child under my care has vanished.

Do they think it again?

Holloway exhales, his voice softer now. "Now, I know you were telling the truth."

It doesn't make me feel any better.

I grip the phone, my breath shaky. "If you know that, then find my son. Because I am not losing him the way I lost them."

Holloway is quiet for a second. Then:

"We'll find him."

I hang up before he can say anything else.

Dan is watching me, his face tight with worry. "Izzy—"

I shake my head, wrapping my arms around myself. "They don't have anything."

He exhales slowly. "They're trying."

I let out a hollow laugh. "Trying isn't enough." I look at him then, my voice shaking. "She's three steps ahead of them. I know it."

Dan rubs a hand over his face, exhaustion pulling at his features. "Then what do we do?"

I stare out the window again. The street is quiet. The cops aren't moving quickly enough. Holloway and Birch are probably sitting at their desks, running searches, making calls, doing everything except finding my son.

I straighten. "We find her ourselves."

Dan blinks. "Izzy—"

"No," I cut him off. "We don't wait. We go."

Because I know Claire, Carrie, better than they do. And I know one thing for certain: if the police don't find her soon, I never will.

I can't sit still. Not while Noah is out there. Not while the police waste precious time on background checks and bureaucratic bullshit.

I press my palms against my temples, pacing the length of the living room, forcing my brain to work, to remember. Think, Izzy. Think.

Claire, Carrie, had been in my life for nearly two years. I had spent hours with her. Trusted her. Let her into my home. She must have said something. Something I missed. Some detail that at the time seemed harmless but is now the key to finding my son.

I close my eyes, willing myself to rewind through every

conversation. Every throwaway comment. Then, like a slap, it hits me.

A rainy afternoon. The two of us sitting at my kitchen table, sipping coffee, talking about dreams, escape, starting over.

"I used to dream about running away to the countryside," Claire had said wistfully, stirring sugar into her mug. "There's this old cabin in Pennysylvania that belongs to my family. We used to go there when I was a kid. Near, Susquehanna Trails. No one else around for miles, just trees and peace. I always thought one day I'd go back and never leave."

I stop pacing, my breath catching in my throat.

Pennysylvania.

I spin toward Dan. "She has a cabin near Susquehanna Trails."

Dan looks up sharply from his laptop, his tired eyes instantly alert. "What?"

"She told me about it once," I say quickly, the words tumbling from my mouth. "Her family had a cabin in the woods. She said she used to go there when she was younger. That it was isolated."

Dan is already grabbing his laptop, his fingers flying over the keyboard. "Where?"

I shake my head. "She never said exactly. Just that it was deep in the woods. Secluded. Off the grid."

Dan mutters a curse under his breath, pulling up a satellite map of Pennysylvania. "Pennysylvania has millions of acres of forest, Izzy." He zooms in, clicking on endless stretches of green, covered in dirt roads and small, hidden trails. "She could be anywhere."

I sit beside him, dragging my own laptop toward me, my fingers trembling as I type into the search bar.

"Remote cabins in Susquehanna Trails."

"Secluded cabins in woods."

"Abandoned family properties."

Dozens of listings pop up, some vacation rentals, some private residences, some old, long-forgotten structures buried deep in the trees.

Too many.

I bite my lip, forcing my thoughts to focus.

“She said it was her family’s,” I murmur, scanning the results. “So it has to be old. Not something newly built. Maybe even something abandoned.”

Dan nods, shifting his search. He pulls up property records, digging through old sales, inherited estates, foreclosures. His brow furrows in concentration.

I keep going, clicking through more articles, more listings, more anything that might give me a clue.

Then I try something else.

"Langley cabin Pennysylvania."

I hit enter.

At first, nothing.

Then, buried beneath real estate articles, a property listing from years ago.

I click on it, my stomach twisting.

A small, rustic cabin in an area near Castle Fin, Sesquehanna Trails. The details are sparse, the photos grainy. But the description catches my eye.

"Off the grid. No direct road access. Previously owned by the Langley family."

Langley.

My pulse pounds against my ribs.

I turn the laptop toward Dan, my finger jabbing at the screen. “That’s it.”

Dan leans in, scanning the listing. His eyes narrow. “It’s

barely even on the map." He clicks over to a satellite view, zooming in. "Look at this. No major roads leading in. You'd have to take back trails. No security cameras. No close neighbors."

I swallow hard.

It's perfect.

Too perfect.

"She planned this," I whisper. "She knew what she was doing."

Dan breathes heavily, rubbing his jaw. "This has to be where she took him."

I don't hesitate. I push my chair back, standing so fast it nearly topples over. "We have to go."

Dan hesitates, his brows furrowing. "Izzy—"

"No," I cut him off. "We don't wait. We go."

He exhales sharply, rubbing a hand over his face. "We should call Birch."

I shake my head violently. "No. If we call them, they'll take too long. They'll say they need a warrant, or they'll spend hours verifying the location." My voice trembles. "We don't have time for that, Dan."

Dan looks at me for a long moment, his expression unreadable.

Then, finally, he nods.

"Let's go."

30

PRESENT

The road vanishes beneath us, swallowed by an endless stretch of darkened trees.

The deeper we go, the more the world narrows. It feels as if civilization has been left behind, no streetlights, no signs of life, just miles of dense, whispering forest pressing in from all sides. The car's headlights carve a thin beam through the darkness, illuminating the winding dirt path that stretches endlessly ahead.

Dan grips the wheel tightly, his knuckles white. The tires crunch over gravel and dead leaves, sending small rocks skittering into the shadows.

Neither of us speaks.

Not because we lack words, because there's too much to say. But what good would it do? We both know why we're here. We both know what we're about to face.

The farther we drive, the tighter the feeling in my chest grows.

This is her place.

The woods around us feel untouched, forgotten like no one has set foot in them for decades. The trees loom high, skeletal against the sliver of moonlight peeking through shifting clouds. Shadows spill across the path, stretching, twisting.

A primal part of me knows we shouldn't be here. That no one should.

Then, through the thick maze of trees, a shape emerges in the distance.

The cabin.

I know it's hers before Dan even slows the car.

It sits hunched against the tree line, small and dark, like it's been waiting for us.

The windows are black, void of any light. The wooden walls are worn down by time and neglect. The porch leans slightly, its railing missing in places. Vines creep up the sides, strangling the structure as if the forest itself is trying to reclaim it.

Dan kills the engine.

The silence that follows is suffocating.

I stare at the cabin, my pulse a steady drum in my ears.

This is where she has my son.

This is where he's been, alone, scared, with her.

Dan inhales deeply, forcing himself to stay calm. "No signal."

I nod. I expected that.

"I'll go back down the road," he says, gripping my hand tightly. "Try to get a call through to Birch." His jaw tightens. "Promise me you won't go inside."

I swallow hard, forcing myself to nod.

It's a lie.

Dan exhales, watching me carefully. "Izzy—"

"I promise," I whisper.

His eyes search mine, then finally, reluctantly, he nods. He presses a kiss to my forehead before disappearing into the trees, his figure swallowed almost instantly by the dark.

The second he's gone, I turn back to the house. The forest seems to hold its breath. And then I step forward.

The steps groan under my weight as I move toward the door. The wood is damp, soft at the edges, nearly rotting. The air is thick with the scent of wet earth and something else, something stale and forgotten.

I press a hand against the door. It gives too easily, the hinges barely holding on.

The moment I step inside, the temperature drops.

The air is wrong in here.

Still. Heavy. *Watching.*

A thick layer of dust coats the floor, except for a set of fresh footprints leading deeper into the house. Faint traces of candle wax stain the wooden planks near the doorway.

The furniture is sparse. An old couch, its fabric torn; a wooden table, one leg slightly uneven; a fireplace, empty except for a pile of cold ashes.

But beyond the silence, beyond the stillness I hear her.

The soft, familiar hum of her voice.

Claire. Carrie.

The sound slithers under my skin. It's low and sweet, a melody meant to soothe as I creep forward, my breath shallow, my pulse hammering.

The sound grows louder.

I round the corner and see them.

Carrie sits in a worn rocking chair in the back room, bathed in the dim glow of a dwindling fire. The light flickers against the walls, dancing across her face.

She cradles Noah in her lap.

His small body is curled into her, his face pressed against her shoulder. His arms hang limp at his sides, his little fingers twitching in his sleep. His eyelashes are damp, sticking to his cheeks.

My breath catches in my throat. I make a sound, something feral and unintentional.

Noah stirs. His head lifts, his little face twisting in confusion and then his eyes find me. For a second, he is still. Then he bolts.

He scrambles out of Carrie's arms, his feet hitting the floor with a thud, his body launching toward me with a strangled sob.

"Mommy!"

But Carrie is faster.

She catches his arm before he can reach me. Noah whimpers, his small body trembling. His fingers flex toward me, desperate. Carrie doesn't look at him. She looks at me. And she smiles.

"Oh, Izzy." Her voice is warm, almost pleased. "You worked it out."

A cold shiver slides down my spine. My mouth is dry. My hands are shaking. But I force my voice to steady.

"Let him go."

Carrie tilts her head, her expression almost pitying like I'm the one who doesn't understand.

She kneels beside Noah, brushing his curls back from his damp cheeks.

"Don't be scared, Little One." Her voice is soft, soothing. She strokes his hair, her fingers lingering. "Mommy's here."

Noah sobs. "No!" He tries to pull away, tries to run to me but Carrie holds on.

I take a step closer, my pulse pounding.

"Let. Him. Go."

Carrie lifts her head, her smile fading.

And for the first time her eyes change. The warmth, the false kindness drops. And something darker settles in its place. Something twisted.

"You don't deserve him, Isabel." Her voice is calm. Sure. "He's better off here. With me."

The room spins. And in that moment, I know. This woman will not let my son go without a fight.

The fire crackles weakly in the hearth, the only source of warmth in the decaying cabin. The air is thick with the scent of damp wood, mildew, and something else, something old and musty, like fabric that hasn't been aired out in years.

The walls are bare, the paint peeling in long, curling strips, revealing brittle wood beneath. The single rocking chair still creaks gently where Carrie had been sitting moments ago, a ghostly rhythm in the tense silence.

The rest of the room is sparse.

An old table stands in the corner, its surface coated in dust, except for a small, neat spot where a plate sits, a half-eaten sandwich abandoned beside a glass of milk. A worn rug covers part of the wooden floor, its edges frayed, chewed away by time or pests.

This place isn't a home. It's a shrine to something long dead.

Noah trembles in Carrie's grasp, his small fingers still stretched toward me. His curls are messy, damp with sweat, his cheeks stained with dried tears. His little body is stiff, his chest rising and falling in rapid, shallow breaths.

Carrie, by contrast, is eerily still. Her face is pale, almost waxy in the dim light.

Her eyes, once so familiar, so friendly, are now dark and hollow, locked onto mine with a quiet, simmering intensity. She looks thinner than before, her cheekbones sharper, her lips cracked, like she's been forgetting to eat or drink. Her hair, usually neat and styled, is wild, tangled at the edges.

She doesn't look like the woman I knew. *She looks possessed.* And I know now I can't win through force.

She's too far gone. Too deep inside her own mind, her own delusions and if I fight her, she'll fight back.

"I knew you'd come," she says, her voice soft, almost tender.

I swallow hard and force my voice to steady. "You don't want to hurt him, Carrie."

She doesn't move.

I glance at Noah again, my body screaming to run to him, to grab him, take him home. But I don't move. Not yet. Not while she's still standing between us.

Carrie sighs, almost wistfully. "You don't understand, do you?"

I clench my fists. "Understand what?"

She exhales, shaking her head. "You always do this, Izzy. You never see what's right in front of you."

Something sharp and cold digs into my chest. She says my name like she's known me forever. Like she has the right.

I don't respond. I can't. Instead, I stare at her, waiting.

Carrie presses her lips together, her fingers twitching at her sides, as if resisting the urge to reach for me, to make me understand.

"I saved him," she says finally, her voice soft but resolute. "I saved him from you."

My pulse pounds in my ears. I take a step forward, but she doesn't flinch.

"No," I breathe. "You took him. You stole him."

She shakes her head. "I gave him a chance. A chance that Theo and Charlotte never had."

Ice floods my veins. She says their names so casually, so easily.

Theo. Charlotte.

Names that still feel like glass against my skin, like something broken that can never be put back together.

Carrie knew them.

My breath catches. "Who... who are you?"

She laughs, quiet, breathy, as if this is some inside joke I'm too slow to understand.

"Oh, Izzy," she murmurs. "You don't even remember, do you?"

She steps closer. I force myself not to move, not to retreat, even though every part of me screams to run.

"I was there," she continues, her voice gentle. "I was there when it happened. I was there when those poor children were forgotten, left behind, discarded like they didn't matter."

I shake my head, but the world tilts beneath me.

No. No, that's not true. *I loved them.*

Carrie's smile fades, her expression shifting into something rawer, more dangerous.

"They never should have been in that house," she hisses. "You know that, don't you? You knew how their parents were. You knew how little they cared. And yet, you left them."

My breath shudders.

"I didn't—"

"You turned your back for one second, and they were gone." She cuts me off.

Her voice is sharp now, edged with something wild, something that's been waiting to come out.

My stomach twists.

"They drowned," I whisper.

Carrie's expression turns to steel. "No, they were abandoned."

A ragged breath escapes her lips. She's unraveling now, her careful composure cracking at the edges.

"I watched," she continues, her eyes burning. "I watched from the sidelines, just like I always did, while people like you played house with children that weren't even yours."

She steps forward, and suddenly, I can't breathe.

"You weren't fit to take care of them," she seethes. "And neither was their mother. And neither are you now."

Her words cut like a blade straight to the heart.

I swallow, my throat tight. "You... you think I hurt them?"

Her laugh is hollow. "You didn't have to. You were weak. You were the girl who never quite fit, never quite belonged, never had the strength to fight for them."

I blink. And suddenly, it all clicks into place.

Her voice. Her obsession. Her anger. She was there. Not just watching. Not just some stranger in the shadows. She was part of it.

"You knew Oliver," I say slowly, reminding her.

She stills. Her eyes narrow.

I take another step forward, the fear in my chest replaced with something cold, sharp, unforgiving.

"You were part of their lives," I murmur. "You... loved them."

Carrie's breath stutters. Then, finally, she nods.

"Yes," she whispers. "I loved them."

Her voice cracks.

"But they were never mine."

The confession hangs between us, heavy and suffocating.

I shake my head, my vision blurring. "So you took my son?"

Carrie exhales, a quiet, trembling sound.

"I saved him."

She believes it. She truly, honestly believes it. And suddenly, I understand. This isn't just about Noah. This isn't just about revenge. This is about redoing the past. She couldn't save Theo and Charlotte. So she's trying to save him. I swallow the bile rising in my throat, forcing my voice to stay steady.

"You're wrong," I whisper. "You didn't save him."

Carrie blinks, her body swaying slightly, like something inside her is breaking.

I press forward.

"You stole him," I say. "And now, you're going to lose again."

Her breathing stutters. Her face contorts. Her hands clench into fists, her whole body trembling.

"No," she rasps. "No, not this time."

Her eyes flick toward Noah. I take a sharp step forward.

"Noah," I say, my voice loud, **firm**, cutting through the madness like a knife.

He looks at me, his little face crumpling.

In that moment, I see the fear in his eyes. The same fear I've been drowning in. The same fear that proves she's lying.

I take a slow, cautious step forward. I have to handle this differently.

"You just want to protect him."

For the first time, her grip on Noah falters.

Just slightly.

A flicker of something crosses her face that looks like a moment of doubt. I seize it.

Lowering myself carefully to my knees, I put myself level with her, making myself small.

"I know what you're trying to do," I whisper. "You tried to save Theo and Charlotte, right?"

She flinches. Her lips part, but no sound comes out.

I press on.

"But look what happened to them." My throat tightens. "Do you really want Noah to end up like them?"

Carrie stiffens, her breath hitching. A shadow crosses her face, something raw and painful cracking through her expression. Her eyes dart to Noah, her fingers twitching at his arm. She's seeing him now. Not as the child she wants him to be. Not as the one she lost. But as him. Noah. A little boy who is scared and cold and just wants to go home.

Carrie's lips tremble. Her face twists in anguish.

"I never meant—" Her voice cracks, barely more than a whisper.

Her hand shakes. Then, finally she lets go.

Noah bolts, launching himself into my arms with a sob. His small body collides into mine, and I wrap him up, holding him so tightly I can feel his heartbeat hammering against my ribs.

I close my eyes, inhaling the scent of his hair, his warmth, his life.

He's here.

He's safe.

Carrie doesn't move.

She just stares at her empty hands, her breathing ragged, her entire body trembling as if she's only just realizing what she's done.

As if, for the first time, she sees *herself.* She lets out a sob—a raw, strangled sound.

"I just wanted to make it right," she whispers.

The past has finally caught up to her. And this time, she won't escape it.

The air inside the cabin is suffocating.

Thick with the scent of mildew and burning wood, heavy with dust and something older, something rotting. The weak fire casts flickering shadows across the walls, making everything seem alive, as if the house itself is breathing.

Carrie kneels on the floor in front of me, her entire body trembling, her sobs broken and raw. It's the kind of crying that comes from somewhere deep where pain festers, where wounds never heal.

Her fingers dig into the wooden floorboards, her nails scraping against the dirt-caked crevices. Her breath comes in sharp gasps, her shoulders rising and falling violently.

"I only ever wanted to save them," she whispers.

Her voice is barely more than a breath, but the words settle over the room like a curse.

Noah clings to me, his little hands twisted in my sweater, his body trembling against mine. I tighten my hold on him, pressing his face into my shoulder so he can't see her like this, so he can't hear what she's about to say.

But he hears it. I know he hears it. Because when she speaks again, her voice is cold, detached.

"I tried to take Charlotte first."

The words slice through the air, jagged and sharp.

My stomach churns.

"She was so small. So perfect." Carrie tilts her head slightly, her lips twitching at the corners in something that almost resembles a smile. "She should have been mine."

I swallow hard, forcing myself to stay still, to keep my breathing steady. I don't say anything. I can't. Because if I do, I'll shatter.

Carrie breathes shakily, her gaze unfocused, lost in some memory I don't want to see. "But Theo wouldn't let me." She lets out a choked laugh, humorless and brittle. "He fought me. Screamed, cried... he wouldn't let her go."

The horror of her words sinks into my skin like ice. I try to block out the images forming in my head, but I can't.

31

Theo—a little boy no older than Noah—fighting for his sister, fighting against Carrrie.

I taste bile rising in the back of my throat.

Carrie presses a trembling hand to her temple, rocking slightly. "I didn't want to hurt him," she says, voice raw. "I didn't." She shakes her head violently. "But he wouldn't stop. He wouldn't—" She lets out a sharp breath, her eyes suddenly wide, panicked. "I had to make him quiet. I had to."

My chest tightens. The air feels thinner, as if the walls are closing in and Noah lets out a whimper against my shoulder.

Carrie's face twists, her mouth opening and closing, as if she's trapped inside the memory, inside that moment.

"The water was so cold," she murmurs. "He struggled at first. But after a while..." Her voice trails off, her lips parting in something almost like wonder. "He just... stopped."

I feel my body sway, my grip on Noah tightening as my vision blurs.

This can't be real. It can't.

"But Charlotte," Carrie continues, her voice sharp again.

"She was different." She lets out a breathy laugh. "She screamed. She fought." Her head tilts again, her eyes glowing with something unnatural. "She wouldn't stop crying. She wouldn't call me Mommy."

Carrie presses her nails into her arms, deep enough to leave marks.

"She should have known," she whispers.

I don't realize I'm shaking until I feel Noah's little fingers digging into my side, clinging to me like a lifeline.

Carrie looks up then, meeting my gaze fully for the first time since she started talking.

And I see it. The truth.

The thing I always knew deep down, even when I didn't want to admit it. Someone killed them. *She killed them.*

She wanted to take Charlotte, to raise her as her own. But when it didn't work. When Charlotte refused to accept her as her mother, she drowned her, just like she drowned Theo.

I feel like I'm going to be sick. A loud noise shatters the tension. The distant wail of sirens.

Carrie's head jerks up. Her body goes rigid.

Flashing lights slice through the cracks in the wooden slats, beams of white piercing the dimly lit cabin. The low rumble of voices, the heavy sound of boots crunching over gravel.

The police. They're here.

For a moment, hope flares in my chest. But then Carrie moves.

She stands abruptly, her breathing ragged, her eyes darting between me, Noah, and the door. She knows it's over. But something in her gaze, something twisted and desperate, tells me she isn't going to let it end the way I want it to.

Slowly, she reaches into her pocket.

My blood runs cold.

I know what she's about to do before I even see the blade. The knife is old, worn, but its edge still gleams, sharp enough to cut. Firelight flickers across the steel as she lifts it, turning it in her hands.

I step back instinctively, my arms tightening around Noah.

"Carrie." My voice is barely a whisper.

She tilts her head, smiling.

"You took everything from me," she murmurs.

Her grip on the knife tightens.

"First Evelyn." Her eyes darken. "And now you."

Her lips curve upward.

"But I win," she breathes.

A terrible, twisted realization settles over me. She isn't going to fight me. She isn't going to run. She's going to make this her choice. Her victory.

I lurch forward, reaching out instinctively. "Carrie, don't—"

She steps back. A soft, breathy laugh escapes her lips. She looks at Noah one last time.

"Take care of him," she whispers.

Her eyes are glassy.

"Mommy loves you, Little One."

And before I can stop her, before I can move, Carrie lifts the knife to her throat and drags it *across her skin.*

A sickening, wet sound fills the room. Blood spills instantly, thick and dark, cascading down the front of her dress in violent, pulsing waves. Her body jerks, knees buckling as she staggers back.

For a brief second, she stands. Then she collapses. She crumples like a broken doll, limbs folding awkwardly beneath her. Her eyes remain open, locked onto the ceiling. Empty.

Noah screams. The door bursts open. Voices. Yelling. Arms grab me, pull me back. I barely register them. I barely register anything. Because all I can see is Carrie lying in a pool of her own blood. Her chest rises once. Then nothing. Her smile lingers, frozen.

It's over. But the horror will never leave us.

EPILOGUE

It has been a week since the cabin. Seven days since the nightmare ended. Seven days since Carrie Langley bled out on the floor, whispering her final words: Mommy loves you, Little One. Seven days since we brought Noah home. But home doesn't feel like home anymore. The house feels wrong. Too big. Too empty. Too quiet.

It used to be filled with warmth and the scent of coffee brewing in the morning, the sound of Noah's laughter echoing through the halls, the reassuring weight of Dan's hand on my back as he passed me in the kitchen.

Now, the air inside these walls is stale, heavy. Like we left something behind in that cabin, something we can't quite recover.

Noah hasn't been the same since we brought him back.

At night, I hear his small footsteps pacing across the upstairs hallway, restless long after he should be asleep. He doesn't play like he used to. He no longer races his toy cars across the floor, making engine sounds, or begs to go to the park. He barely speaks at all.

He's distant. It's like he's here, *but not really here.* And I don't know how to fix it.

This morning, I found him curled up in the corner of his room, clutching his stuffed rabbit, staring at the wall. His tiny fingers gripped the fabric so tightly his knuckles had turned white.

When I asked if he wanted breakfast, he didn't answer. He didn't even look at me.

I sat beside him, brushing his curls from his forehead, whispering his name. Still, nothing. It's as if he's trapped inside his own head, locked away in a place I can't reach. And I wonder, what did Carrie say to him when I wasn't there? What words did she plant in his mind?

I don't ask Dan if he notices it too. I already know he does. Because he's not the same either. Dan has barely looked at me since that night. He tries to hide it and tries to act like everything is fine, like we're moving forward.

But I see it. The flicker of sadness in his eyes. The tightness in his jaw when I enter a room. The way his hand hesitates before reaching for mine. Like I'm someone he can't quite trust.

I know why. I promised him I wouldn't go into the cabin. And I did. I told him I would wait. And I lied. And now, even though he doesn't say it, I know he wonders what if I hadn't? What if I had just listened? Would Carrie still be alive? Would Noah be better? Would we be better?

But I don't regret it. Not for a second. Because if I had waited, if I had let the police handle it, who knows what would have happened?

Would Carrie have run? Would she have hurt Noah before they got there? Would she have taken him somewhere else, somewhere I never would have found him?

I don't know. And I never will.

All I know is that I got him back.

But at what cost?

The walls feel thinner now. The bed feels colder.

Dan and I lie next to each other at night, both awake, both silent. His body is right there, inches away, but it may as well be a thousand miles.

We don't talk about it. We don't talk about her. We don't talk about the cabin, or the blood, or the way Noah screamed when Carrie collapsed to the floor. Instead, we go through the motions.

We make dinner. We sit across from each other at the table, barely speaking. We check on Noah, knowing full well he won't say anything. And when we touch, it feels forced like something we're both trying to remember how to do.

The police came by yesterday. Birch and Holloway. They said all the right things. That we were safe. That it was over. That Carrie had no living family, no one to come after us. That we could heal now. But healing isn't that simple. Because the damage isn't on the outside. It's inside. In the quiet moments when I hear something creak in the house and my heart leaps to my throat, convinced she's back. In the way Noah stares out the window sometimes like he's waiting for her. In the way Dan turns away from me in bed, not out of anger, but out of something worse. Something that feels like regret.

I don't know if things will ever go back to how they were. I don't know if they can.

I think about her more than I should. Even now, even knowing what she did, what she was, I can't stop wondering. Was anything real?

The friend I trusted. The woman who sat in my kitchen, who held my son's hand when he tripped at the playground, who laughed with me over too many glasses of wine. Was any of it real? Or was she always this monster, hiding in plain sight?

I try to remember every conversation we ever had, combing

through the details for signs I missed. Did she ever tell the truth? About anything? Was she ever really from upstate New York? Did she really have a sister she no longer spoke to? Did she actually hate her boss, or was that a lie too?

I'll never know. And that's what haunts me the most, the not knowing. Because what if, beneath all the lies and manipulations, she wasn't just evil?

What if she was just... broken?

Not a monster. Just a damaged person who lost something and never recovered.

I don't forgive her. I never will.

But I do wonder. I wonder if she sat across from me all those times, desperate to be something else, something normal, to hold onto the life she had created before it all unraveled.

If there was a version of Claire—Carrie—that was real. If, in some way, she actually did love Noah. And that thought? That's the part that keeps me awake at night.

Because if she did, even a little, then maybe she wasn't lying when she told him, Mommy loves you, Little One. And I know my son heard her. I know he believed her.

The thought makes my chest ache, makes my stomach twist with something ugly. Because if Noah loved her back, if even the smallest part of him misses her, then maybe I really did lose him, just a little. And maybe I'll never get him back.

The house is silent now.

Dan has already gone to bed, but I can't sleep. I never can. Not now.

The nights are the worst. Too quiet, too still, too open to the thoughts I try so hard to push away. So, I do what I always do. I check on Noah. I move through the hallway on autopilot, my bare feet whispering against the wooden floors.

The doors are all locked. The windows shut. The security system armed.

I check them all anyway. Because the fear never goes away. Because sometimes, when I close my eyes I still see her. The way she looked at him. The way she spoke to him. The way she smiled, so sure, so certain, as if she had already won.

My pulse pounds as I reach Noah's room. I barely register opening the door, barely feel the cool air against my skin as I step inside. And then I see him. Sitting up in bed, his small frame barely making a dent in the mattress. His back is straight, his hands resting limply in his lap. Moonlight slants through the window, casting silver shadows across his face, making him look almost unreal. But it's not his posture that freezes me. It's the sound.

A soft, little hum. The same tune I heard in the cabin. The one Carrie sang to him. The one Claire sang to him.

My breath catches in my throat.

I don't move. I can't.

Noah hums to himself, rocking slightly, his eyes unfocused.

Ice creeps up my spine, my body going rigid with something I can't name.

"Noah?" I whisper.

The humming stops.

Slowly, he turns to look at me. His eyes are big and dark, lost in shadow. Unreadable. For a long moment, he doesn't speak.

Carrie is still here.

Not in body. Not in flesh. But in the spaces she left behind. In the parts of Noah's mind I can't reach. She got inside him.

Noah blinks at me. Then he nods, slowly, as if remembering what he's supposed to do. He's meant to be sleeping.

I tuck him back in, pulling the blanket up to his chin. His tiny fingers grip the fabric, his gaze drifting to the ceiling.

I lean down, pressing a kiss to his forehead. "I love you," I whisper.

For a long moment, he says nothing. Then a pause. A hesitation. And finally,

"I love you too, Mommy."

But it doesn't feel real. It feels learned. Rehearsed. Like something he remembers he's supposed to say.

I smooth his hair back, swallowing the lump in my throat.

I know what the police said. Carrie Langley is dead. But I also know the truth.

We will never be free of her. She won. She got what she wanted. Because even in death, she still has a piece of my son.

And then, finally, I ask, "Noah, sweetheart... where did you hear that song?"

But I already know the answer.

Printed in Dunstable, United Kingdom

66309692R00143